THE OUTFIELD

THE OUTFIELD

Out beyond the lands of right
and wrong, there is a field.
I'll meet you there.
Rumi

SHIREEN KALRA

Vitasta

To

My Grandparents

Published by
Renu Kaul Verma
Vitasta Publishing Pvt Ltd
2/15, Ansari Road, Daryaganj
New Delhi - 110 002
info@vitastapublishing.com

ISBN: 978-93-90961-95-5

First Edition 2023
MRP ₹399

This novel is entirely a work of fiction. Names, characters, events and incidents are entirely imaginary. Reference to real places, actual regions, institutions or community practices has been made in a fictitious manner. Any resemblance to actual persons, living or dead or actual events is purely coincidental.

Edited by Nitin Sathe
Typeset & Cover Design by Somesh Kumar Mishra
Printed by Vikas Computer and Printers, New Delhi

Contents

Chapter 1

"A New Era"

Rashika

10 January 1966. New Delhi.

As I see it, there are two kinds of kids rushing out of the primary-wing of Modern School, Barakhamba Road at *chutti* time.

The first kind are kids who go back to their homes in different parts of the national capital and eat lunch at a table where their families discuss the latest political decisions in the country.

The second kind are kids who return to government bungalows located in the North-Eastern end of India Gate and eat lunch at tables where their politician fathers and their colleagues of the power corridor make those political decisions.

My friend Veer Pratap Singh and I belong to the second category. As children of Congress ministers, our lives revolve around Indian politics. Little did we know that today our lives were about to change forever.

The bell rings, and school is over for the day. Veer and I pick up our identical red bags and race each other to the main gate, where, as always, our driver Prem Uncle is waiting to pick us up in the white Ambassador. We climb into the backseats and begin telling him all about our day at school. How we sang the national anthem in the morning assembly after Principal sir hoisted the tri-colour flag. How *motichoor* ladoos were distributed during lunchtime. How our teachers were so happy that most of them didn't even give us any homework.

Mom and Dad had also seemed particularly cheerful when I greeted them this morning. Dad had lifted me in his arms and told me to remember today's date.

'Today marks a new era of peace within the Indian subcontinent,' he'd said. Mom, too, hummed while ironing her lovely silk saree for the celebratory dinner for Congress families at Indira Madam's place that night.

Shastri uncle's trip to the USSR has been the only topic of discussion during family dinners for the past month. With the signing of the Tashkent Decleration today, the war with Pakistan has formally ended. The whole country seems to be celebrating his success.

On our drive back home, Vijay Chowk, Rajpath, and the roads of our locality were all being decorated with flowers.

Our car stops in front of our adjacent houses—15 and 16 Akbar Road. Huge white bungalows with red brick boundary walls as high as the towering black gates. The civics textbook calls our neighborhood of government residences a hallmark of Lutyens' Delhi.

Before heading inside, Veer and I decide to meet at my house in half an hour and listen to the weekly episode of *Geetmala* on the radio.

I'd just finished lunch when Veer and his mother, Gaytri Aunty, enter the living room. Gaytri Aunty has the latest issue of *Sarita* in her hands. Mom fetches coal embers for the kangri and joins her on the sofa.

Veer and I sit on the woolen carpet and switch on the radio. I adjust the antenna for the signal while he tunes into *Geetmala*. *Titli Udi Ud ke Chali* is playing at number four this week. Given the country's mood, I find most songs on the playlist rather peppy.

Geetmala has only reached the seventh song of the day when Lata Didi's melodious voice singing *Piya Tose Naina Lage Re* is interrupted abruptly and replaced by noisy interference. I'm trying to adjust the antenna again, thinking it to be a signal problem when the news anchor's voice suddenly crackles over the speakers…

The magazine in our mothers' hands drops to the floor when they hear the announcement. They rise in utter disbelief and cup their hands over their gasping mouths.

'...Prime Minister Lal Bahadur Shastri…is no more.'

For the first time in my life, I'm sad to get an extra holiday from school.

India is in mourning. The Indian flag that was flying high over State buildings yesterday is at half-mast. Melancholy classical music dominates all radio channels.

Veer and I have been sitting on the porch for most of the morning, waiting for our parents to return from the State funeral. As we hear multiple cars halting, we run towards the gate. They're back!

Mom and Gaytri Aunty get out of the first car. Their white sarees are wrinkled, and their eyes appear swollen. Dad and other neighbours get out of the vehicles that follow.

'Gulzari ji will not be PM for long…the party will hold fresh parliamentary elections soon enough.' We hear Dad tell Mom as they make their way into the house.

'Who do you think the leadership will back this time?' Mom asks.

'From what I have heard, the leadership looks divided...between Morarji Sahib and Indira ji. It'll be a tough call.'

No move takes place in Congress without the prior

approval of these elderly party leaders. Winning the support of these old uncles is absolutely essential. Even *we* know this. And we're just eleven years old.

Our English teacher tells us children to be curious. But Dad gets angry when I ask questions. 'Rashika, politics is not a child's cup of tea,' he says.

I don't think he knows that Veer and I overhear political 'tea' all the time. From cook bhaiya and Asha Didi to *mali* uncle and the guards at Veer's house, no one ever gets tired of talking politics. Veer says he's good at knowing things that the adults don't want us to. When I grow up and become a journalist, his talent will come in handy.

In the next few hours, as Veer and I silently play a game of snakes and ladders in the courtyard, his dad, Vikram Uncle, gets summoned to Morarji Sahib's house.

Back at my house, Dad and two of his friends are busy drafting letters and making phone calls.

'...so can Madam count on your full support then?' Dad repeats multiple times on the phone that night. And then night after night for the next few days.

It is 19th January, nine days from the time the bad news rocked the country. I find Dad sitting contentedly at the dining table having his dinner and not glued to the landline for once.

At today's secret ballot election held in the Congress Office, Madam has defeated senior statesman Morarji Sahib by a two-third majority.

Sometime later, Dad and his friends gather in our

garden, sitting around a fire and celebrate her victory. I notice Vikram Uncle is missing from the gathering.

A week later, Mrs Indira Priyadarshini Gandhi takes oath as the new Prime Minister of India.

Chapter 2

"Fine. Stay."

Veer

With my cricket bat in one hand and a ball in the other, I tiptoe past the living room. Rashika and the other kids must already be waiting for me in the neighbourhood park. I must hurry. But I also must not get caught leaving the house.

Dad has been annoyed and out of sorts since he returned from Madam swearing-in ceremony. Who knows how he'd react if he suspects I'm going to play without completing my homework first. I find the door of Dad's study open as I cross the hallway.

Oh no.

I hide behind the pillar, waiting for the right opportunity to run past his study.

Dad is at his desk, dictating some sort of a speech to his steno, under the shadow of the life-size wall portrait of my late grandfather, Prithvi Pratap Singh—freedom fighter and respected leader of the Congress. It was always certain that Dad would join politics one day. However, Dadu's untimely demise compelled Dad to fill his place in the party at a rather young age. It was Dadu's old friend, Morarji Sahib, who took Dad under his wing and helped him navigate the tricky waters during his early years. Dad calls him his political *guru*.

Dad keeps telling me that I too have to carry the mantle of our family legacy of serving the nation when I grow up. I'm not sure if I can do that by playing cricket instead of politics.

It is different for Rashika, though. The Chaudhary's were wealthy zamindars in Uttar Pradesh before independence; before her grandfather decided to support Chacha Nehru's land reform bill and gave up surplus tracts of their ancestral land for the cause of social justice. Later on, Amar Uncle joined the Indian Youth Congress as an advocate for economic equality and worked closely with Mrs Gandhi for a long time.

The steno comes out of Dad's study with his notepad and closes the door behind him. Now is my chance.

It takes me no more than ten seconds to dash from the pillar to the house door and out of the main gate.

When I reach Akbar road park, all my friends are gathered around the muddy pitch for the toss. But wait, where is Rashika?

I look around the park for her. Rashika missing evening cricket can mean only one thing—Amar Uncle has locked her in her room. Yet again. I mean, c'mon! Our exams are in March. It's only January!

'Don't start just yet, I'll get Rashika!' I tell my friends.

'Veer, it's okay, we have enough players to make two teams,' Inder, the captain of our opponent team replies.

'No. I'll quickly go and get her.'

'You always do this Veer! And when you don't come back, we lose our best player!' my teammate Bunty complains.

'You are the best player Bunty!' I reassure him as I run towards Rashika's house.

There is no way I'm playing without my opening partner.

Seeing how fast I can climb up the water pipe to Rashika's room on the first floor, I agree with Pooja ma'am. Humans have indeed evolved from chimpanzees.

When I knock, Rashika comes to the window at once like she was expecting me.

'C'mon, let's go. We have a very important match. Maths can wait.' I declare, jumping into her room.

'Veer, I can't!' she gives me the answer I've heard a hundred times before.

'Yes you can.' I try to convince her. 'No one will know Rashika. We'll just quietly climb down the pipe. I promise I'll have you back in your room before Amar

Uncle comes back.'

'I'm sorry, I can't. Dad was very clear. I can't step out of the room until all the word problems are solved.' She is stubborn. 'You go play!'

'Not without you.'

'Veer, we'll lose if you don't play!'

'We won't. Bunty can handle that.' I say bouncing on her bed.

'Veer, seriously, go!' she insists, pulling me up.

'No point. I'll get out running between the wickets with anyone else!' I bounce back. It is a well-practiced routine.

'Fine. Stay.' She rolls her eyes at me, before closing the window.

'Now, let's solve those stupid word problems, and get them over with quickly.' I take my usual seat on the side of her desk.

Chapter 3

"Every Election Is Important"

Veer

1967. The fourth General Elections are only a month away.

While any usual household may be the busiest around a wedding or a festival, a political household is definitely the busiest around the time of elections—the festival of democracy. For us political families, elections are THE event of the year. And the year before. And the year after it.

Dad says that every election is important. But looking at how hard everyone is working this time, I'd say that this election appears extra important.

I see people gathering in our front lawn the whole day, waiting for a quick word with Dad. As he greets them with folded arms, they fall over each other to put marigold garlands around his neck. He then patiently listens to their grievances before heading to the party office. Each day, as he arrives back home from work, he looks worn out. Yet again, the next day, he has to go to attend some meeting or the other.

The scene is similar at Rashika's house. Both our Dads are, once again, contesting for the Lok Sabha election. Dad is contesting from Dadu's previous constituency, Chandni Chowk, while Amar Uncle is contesting from West Delhi. Most of the older uncles of the party are, as always, contesting from their original 'permanent' constituencies.

I wonder how they still have so much energy to do so many things! For the past month, every radio interview has kept going on and on about how it will not be easy for the Congress this time. Chacha Nehru's charisma is missing, and Mrs Gandhi is new on the job. Not to mention the opposition parties have all united under the socialist leader Ram Manohar Lohia.

Rashika and I find the election season thoroughly entertaining. The clutter of posters and pamphlets. The hustle and bustle of the youth Congress workers running errands and planning rallies. The workers spend so much time at our home, they begin to feel like extended family. Throughout the day, cooks in the kitchen repeat rounds of *Roohafza* and tea for them. Few of them take out time to play cricket with us in the evening. Rashika and I love to wave party flags from atop open trucks and tempos decorated for procession rallies.

Yesterday, Dad took me to Mrs Gandhi's rally at

the Ram Leela Maidan. He wanted me to experience an election campaign first-hand. Rashika also wanted to come, but Amar Uncle refused to let her go without him. So, upon reaching home, I described to her all about the mammoth crowds bursting in applause at Madam's powerful speech on social reform. I also told her how mesmerized I was throughout the event that I didn't leave Dad's side even for a second.

Prasar Bharti will declare the election results anytime now. Everyone in the household is glued to the radio in the drawing-room, waiting for the announcements to begin. Groups of enthusiastic youth workers are already outside our houses with *dhols, malas* and *mithai.*

The broadcast starts. One by one the anchor announces the winning candidate from each constituency. The Congress appears to be winning so far. But we hear the names of other parties too in between…

It is time for the results of the union territory of New Delhi now. Mom is pacing up and down the room, chanting a silent prayer…

Within the very next minute, sounds of drums and slogans begin reverberating on Akbar road. Both Dad and Amar Uncle have won! There is happiness all around.

Mom is relieved as she takes me in her arms. But as the anchor announces the results for the constituencies of Maharashtra...Bengal...Madras...her smile grows weaker, as do the drum beats outside our house.

The elderly stalwarts of the party like SK Patil and Atulya Ghosh and Kamraj who hold commanding positions in the party organisation have lost their seats, one after the other. The Congress party seems to be winning without its original leadership.

I look out through the drawing-room window. Drums outside our house are now silent. However, the drums outside Rashika's home continue loudly. Party workers are joyously dancing around Akbar road.

By the look on the faces of those inside our drawing-room, I doubt this celebration will last for too long.

Chapter 4

"It's Us Versus Them Now"

Veer

From what I've learnt so far, things are bound to get ugly whenever the demise of a beloved old leader is announced on All India Radio.

23 August 1969.

A lot has changed around here in the past two years. Mrs Gandhi is now the people's Prime Minister. She is super popular amongst the poor. She has to be, given all her social policies that make the headlines every other week. For the first time, Congress is losing elections in many states, which apparently, is something to worry about.

Oh! And also, Morarji Sahib was deputy PM, but he ended up resigning last month. You should have seen Dad's face when he got the telegram.

Things are not the same at Akbar road either.

Dad is now a Minister of State for Agriculture and Farmers' Welfare, which is a demotion from his portfolio of Cabinet Minister of Rural Development in the last government. In fact, we were going to shift to a newly allotted residence on Safdarjung road. But, thank God, Amar Uncle intervened and stopped us from moving. He is now the Cabinet Minister of Commerce and Industry, and has a lot more cars and guards following him around.

Both our fathers still come to meet each other sometimes, but those are usually work-related conversations. They don't really laugh or drink together anymore. Rama Aunty also doesn't visit Mom that often. Family dinners at the Chaudhary's are also a thing of the past.

Our families now sit at different tables during party dinners. I have to sit at the boring table with the families of those old uncles from the leadership. Rashika sits at the more prominent 'VIP' table with the Gandhi family and families of younger uncles who have kids our age. That table looks more happening from where we sit.

Rashika and I are still good friends, of course, but we prefer to play in the park now instead of our houses.

Why?

I'm not exactly sure.

So much has been happening that it's hard for me to keep track. And honestly, it isn't as fun anymore. Like right now, I'm trying to complete my homework, but the voices of Mom and Dad arguing are echoing in my room.

'...then how come he won?!' Mom asks, bewildered.

'Due to Indira's support…how else!' Dad answers.

'...but…wasn't Sanjiva Reddy the official party candidate?'

'Exactly! Nijalingappa ji even issued a whip, making it crystal clear who we supported…and yet they all voted for Giri! Cause Indira favours him,' Dad sounds frustrated. 'They defied a direct party order for her… and what the hell is a conscience vote, huh?'

Four months after President Zakir Hussain's death, the race to replace his position is finally over. VV Giri has won the election for the President today afternoon. An election that will hammer the final nail into the coffin of the Indian National Congress.

'Why don't you talk to Chaudhary ji?' Mom suggests, 'Clear things out...there must be a way for reconciliation.'

'Reconciliation?' Dad scoffs, 'Don't you see what they're doing!? There is nothing to clear out...this…this is what Chaudhary...what all of them want...to take away power from the Syndicate.'

'But you can't afford to alienate Indira's faction...she is your Prime Minister! You people *chose* her as Prime Minister...'

'The leadership chose Indira because they saw in her an obedient daughter who'd ask for their advice before making decisions...but since her election, they're losing their voice in the party. We're becoming irrelevant, Gaytri. Of course, we feel betrayed!'

'...then talk to Morarji Sahib, make sure things go your way…'

'And say what? Let's try to fix things with the lady who took away the finance ministry from you and then went on to nationalise banks? They're talking about placing ceilings on income and on property! They want to abolish privy purses, for God's sake! There's no way the syndicate will agree to that.'

'Can you at least try...' Mom persists.

'I could, but it's a dead-end Gaytri...Morarji Sahib won't budge, neither would the others. It's us versus them now. It's unavoidable. The leadership will not stand this fascist behaviour,' Dad declares, 'They have to retaliate, or else they'll lose all authority. There will be consequences. Soon. You'll see!'

Consequences there were...although I did not understand who ended up getting punished.

12 November 1969.

Rashika and I have been waiting at the school gate under the searing sun for the past thirty minutes. Prem Uncle isn't here to pick us yet, which is weird because he is never late. I have never met a more punctual person than him. In fact, he is the one scolding us when we're running late for school every other morning.

We've just finished having a *kulfi* from the *redi* outside (Rashika gets a kick keeping *chillar* in her pant pocket) when Prem uncle finally arrives in the Ambassador.

'Sorry baccha log!' he apologises as we climb into the backseat, 'It's not my fault, I was on time! There was so much traffic...cars, police, and media people outside the

Congress office…'

'And you wouldn't imagine what happened today!' he continues excitedly.

…and here comes our daily dose of political drama.

I know there was some meeting of the All India Congress Committee this afternoon. It was all over the broadcast. But those are usually about logistical stuff, and boring—nothing much to be excited about.

'What?' Rashika asks eagerly.

'Err, you sure you want to know?' he double-checks.

'Yes, of course!'

As if we'd ever say no. We *always* want to know. What happens at the Congress office these days determines how our Dads' mood will be in the evening and also translates into whether or not our mothers will let us go and play.

'I think it's best if sahabs only tell you...*bhaiya*, I do not want to say anything wrong to you both.'

'C'mon Prem Uncle, tell us na,' I plead.

'Please,' Rashika resonates.

'Okay…okay...' Prem Uncle takes in an audible breath, the same way we do before getting our maths test marks from ma'am.

'Congress party split in two,' he announces.

'What do you mean, *split in two?*' I ask, perplexed.

'The party got officially divided into two parts...the leadership expelled Gandhi Madam from the party and then...'

'They what!?' Rashika interrupts, jumping in her seat.

'Listen first *baba*...and then…more than half the party members chose to resign and walk out with her.'

'What about our dads...did they walk out too?' I inquire, afraid to hear the answer I am almost sure of.

'Amar Sahib did...I saw him outside the party office... About Vikram Sahib…I'm not so sure.'

Of course, he didn't. Dad is loyal to the old uncles. There's no chance he would have left.

'But Dad can come back tomorrow, right?' Rashika asks innocently.

'*Aree*! You didn't understand…they didn't walk out for a bathroom break! They walked out to become part of the new Congress party under Gandhi Madam!' he explains. 'There are two different Congress parties now, Congress (R)—of Gandhi Madam and her supporters, and Congress (O)—of Morarji Sahib and his supporters.'

'R? O? What does that even mean? Both are Congress, what difference does it make,' Rashika asks in consternation.

'I do not know *beta*…all I know is that everything changes from now on…'

On hindsight, Prem Uncle was right. Everything changed. Everything.

Chapter 5

"You Have To Stop Them"

Rashika

Two mornings later; I wake up to find my world turned upside down. I hear the commotion of furniture moving and vehicles reversing. Looking down the window, I see tempos parked outside Veer's house. At once, I rush out of my room.

Dad is reading the newspaper in the verandah as usual.

CONGRESS SPLITS ON HISTORIC DAY

Indira Gandhi's Congress (R) to rule in coalition with CPI, DMK. Congress (O) to join opposition.

'What is happening?' I ask.

'Nothing...Vikram is moving out,' he answers, still looking into his paper.

'Moving out?! Why?' I feel shivers go down my spine.

'Vikram is in Congress (O) now; he's not a minister anymore. Only ministers get houses on Akbar road. They have to vacate.'

'But...but where are they going?!'

'Oh, I don't know Rashika!' Dad snaps at me, 'Why don't you go inside huh? We'll talk later.'

Instead, I run out of the gate. Tears have welled up in my eyes and the flood gates are about to burst.

It has been hard to contact Veer since the split. He hasn't come to school, and when I'd called his landline, Gaytri Aunty said he was at our classmate Rahul's house. But when I called Rahul, he said Veer was never there.

Media was swarming outside his house during daylight hours and no one would let me step out. I knew something was off, but *this...*

I have to find Veer. I have to beg him to help me change our fathers' minds. I...I...have to do something at least. He can't just leave.

Outside Veer's house, workers are moving furniture into tempos. The drawing-room sofa...the kitchen almirah...Veer's bed. *Oh God, this can't be happening.*

Veer is standing quietly in the corner of his garden with his backpack.

I run to him, attempting to remove his backpack but he takes a step back.

'Veer, listen...we have to make Uncle change his mind...we still can...'

He doesn't say anything. His eyes are red.

I turn to Vikram Uncle and Gaytri Aunty. They're

counting their suitcases.

'Uncle, Aunty...please don't…' They know what I'm going to say.

'It is your Dad's doing *bachha*, not mine,' Vikram Uncle shakes his head.

'Rashika *beta*, go home,' Gaytri Aunty says calmly, placing her hand on my shoulder.

I dash back into my house to plead with Dad.

'You have to do something, please...Dad...get up, please, you have to stop them!' I cry.

'Vikram has made his choice Rashika…there is nothing we can do,' he says calmly, reading his stupid paper without a care in the world.

How can he be so unaffected? Vikram Uncle is his friend. Like Veer is mine.

Just then, I hear noises of vehicles starting and run out.

The doors of the tempos are closed. Gaytri Aunty is already sitting inside their Ambassador. The driver is loading the last suitcase in its dicky. A man is removing their nameplate off the wall. Vikram Uncle is signing some papers as he walks out of the gate. Veer is taking small steps behind him.

'Veer, say bye to Rashika...' Vikram uncle orders as he enters the car.

Veer meekly waves his hand at me, tears finally rolling down his brave face. 'Veer...please…don't go...' I choke as he closes the door on my face.

The police escort jeep starts driving away from the house. Their car is next.

Veer is leaving. Veer is *really* leaving.

Prem Uncle holds me back as I try to...I don't know... bang on the car window...run behind the speeding car...what do you do when your best friend for the past thirteen years is going away?

I do not know what is happening. I don't know anything anymore.

'Sahib wants you inside right now *betiya*...you don't want to create a scene here, please, come...' he drags me back into my house.

The place on the wall where the nameplate—16, Akbar Road. Vikram Pratap Singh, Minister of State—hung for many years, the frame mark stood brighter than the rest of the painted wall.

It wasn't just the Congress party that broke apart that week.

Five Years Later

Chapter 6

"So Not Funny"

Veer

1974, Hindu College, University of Delhi.

I was around fifteen when I realised for the first time that my dream, like my dad, was to attend Hindu College—the most prestigious institute for Political Science Honours in the country.

Dad got dragged into politics early in life and didn't get to enjoy his youth, like one expects to, and so I, his *innocent and obedient* (wink) son, plan to make up for all his lost time by making THE most of my college life.

Today, my first day at Hindu College, is the time I'll see both our dreams start to come true.

Mounting my Enfield bike, I leave home to pick up Imran from his house. Imran Ali Khan, son of Nawab Ahmad Ali Khan of Rampur. An heir without a kingdom, I call him. Imran and I go way back to class eight—my first year at Doon School. We got to know each other better in the many detentions, cleaning the silverware of the school and arranging books. I must thank our teacher for getting the infamous prankster and the underdog together into a lifelong friendship.

Some poor teacher made the mistake of giving us common detention to clean trophies. And so the new underdog at boarding school became buddies with the infamous prankster. The rest is history.

I honk outside Imran's gate. He comes out with a satchel filled with thick books looking like an archaeologist from the Archeological Survey of India. A white kurta, a koti, denim jeans and a pair of specs I know he doesn't need. Is that an actual pen in his koti pocket? Wow.

'What's with the look *Bhaijaan*?' I ask as he mounts the bike.

'Oh, you know, to support my nerdy act. I heard Hindu girls like nerds.'

The moron slash potential playboy has no idea what he's doing pursuing History Honours. But I appreciate the get-up. If not for the surprise raid on his daddy's *purse* by the *socialist* government, Imran would have ended up in a three-piece suit at the London School of Economics.

Good for me, he didn't. I can't afford to lose another best friend.

The previous best friend in question is the daughter of India's beloved politician Amar Chaudhary—a conspirator in the fall of Congress, the *original* one.

I didn't understand their tricks back then, but I do now. How step by step, they kicked out from the government the very people they once called friends and mentors. From hiding and seeking information and battles of ideology, to the victim card, they've played it all. Very meticulously, too, if I may add.

My dad, for instance, Chaudhary's *jigri dost*, first lost his ministership, and then during the 1971 elections, his Lok Sabha seat, and with it every last bit of his power and prestige. The *Garibi Hatao* manifesto combined with the victory in the 1971 war turned Congress (R) into a messiah from heaven, and Mrs Gandhi into the Iron Lady fighting for India's integrity.

Dad hasn't given up though, the opposition parties are more active than ever now. He's busy organising one protest or the other every week. Just yesterday, he took a train to Ahmedabad to join Jayaprakash Narayanan and Morarji Sahib in the Navnirman student protests.

But all this hasn't been easy on him. He drinks pretty often now. Mom says it isn't a big deal, that he's just tensed, and I believe her. My parents are the most honest people I know. If something was wrong, they'd tell me.

We reach college a little early. Hindu is just twenty minutes away from Rajouri Garden, where we live now. South Delhi is out of a sincere powerless politician's budget.

There's still time for our first lecture, so we decide to hang out at Rajan tea stall—the *adda* of Hinduites—where we meet Abhimanyu, a second-year Economics student. We offer him a cigarette of friendship, and he agrees to give us an exclusive tour of the campus.

Walking through the giant college gates and past the

green gardens, the main red building comes clearly into sight. I must have seen the Hindu building a million times, riding past it now and then, and yet, every time I look at this seventy-five-year-old structure, it makes me feel...young...young and ambitious. Finally entering it as a student amplifies these emotions ten times.

We climb up the stairs to the first floor. Imran and Abhimanyu head for their classes and I move towards mine.

My day is going exactly as I'd always imagined in my head.

But then I go through the Political Science class list put up on the floor's notice board, and my eyes pop out and my head goes for a spin.

I've only reached halfway through the list, searching for my roll number at the bottom half when my finger freezes on a name known all too well to me.

`Rashika Chaudhary`

Dear God,
Of all the colleges, in all the countries, all over the world, you had to land Rashika Chaudhary, daughter of Amar Chaudhary, in my college, in my class.
So not funny.

Sincerely,
VPS

College was supposed to be a dream. Not a nightmare.
Damn it.

No, it can't be her. It can't. I repeatedly tell myself as I walk toward the political theory class. What are the odds? She can't be the only girl named Rashika Chaudhary in all of India. But, a little corner of my mind does not believe me. What if it's actually her. Do I *want* it to be her? Pounding against my chest, my heart is preparing for the worst-case scenario as I head towards class.

Scanning the classroom for a familiar face, my eyes fall on a girl sitting on the first bench who I think is Rashika, and I feeze in my footsteps. I just stand there, in the middle of the bloody door, looking at that girl, assessing her, making sure if it is *her*. I mean, yeah, the features match. The same round face, neatly tied hair, the same black eyes, well, she's wearing specs now. The habits match too. There is only one student I've come across who'd open books even before class. Of course, it is her.

Looking at her outfit, anyone could guess that she is a socialist's daughter—a tote bag, beige khaki pants, a plain white cotton shirt. My eyes pause an extra second at her bosom... *okay*... those weren't really there before.

She looks different now...more...feminine...

She looks *pretty* actually. *Whatever.*

I frown, sensing a weirdness in my chest as I walk past her. Her head is buried in her book. Typical Rashika, I almost smile but stop. No. I will not think of the past. I'm determined not to let Rashika's presence affect me in the slightest. No member of the Chaudhary clan is going to get the satisfaction of ruining even a single minute of my life again.

Chapter 7

"Nevermind"

Rashika

You know the feeling when you lose something you know you can't replace. But even then, you keep trying to get it back.

I have found that something today.

Getting to class before time, I choose the perfect seat at the front and straightaway dive into my political theory book. I can socialise after class too. Right now, I must prepare to make an excellent first impression.

Lost in my book, I honestly don't notice when the class fills with students. I'm introducing myself to the girl sitting next to me when Professor Mehta enters.

He gives us a short welcome, introduces himself and his course and then moves straight to the roll call.

Realising that students from all across the country are sitting together in one classroom intimidates and excites me at the same time.

There are too many students in this class. The attendance is taking forever and I'm starting to get a bit bored. It is when Professor finally reaches the alphabet *V* that my boredom jumps out of the window.

'Veer Pratap Singh,' he calls.

'Present sir,' a deep voice from behind me answers.

Desperate to confirm if the voice indeed belongs to who I think it does, I quickly turn my neck to the row besides mine, and when I do, my heart literally stops.

It is *him.*

It is my Veer.

My best friend. My boy next door. In the flesh. In my college. In my class.

Throughout class, my eyes juggle between Professor Mehta, the wall clock, and Veer. One hour of class felt like five to me.

By the time I pack my things, I see Veer already walking out the door. *Shoot.*

I hang my bag over my shoulder and sprint behind, catching up with him in the corridor.

'Veer!' I call out running after him. He doesn't turn. Perhaps he did not hear me. 'VEER!' I call out so loudly that the people walking ahead of me turn. So does Veer.

He stops and turns to face me. *Damn.* Puberty hit him real hard.

I take a moment to have a closer look at him. He is wearing a plain black shirt, simple denim jeans and must be like six feet tall now! His hair is longer, curlier. His cheekbones are sharp, and his Adam's apple is prominent. I have to admit I'm kind of intrigued to see whether the dimples in his smile are still the same.

'Hi!' I say shyly, contemplating the rationality of hugging him. My eyes move from his rolled-up sleeves to his muscular arms, to the curve of his collar bone visible between the one open button of his shirt.

Gulping, I decide against it. We're all grown up now. Hugging him...umm...might be a little awkward. I feel sweat rolling down my temples.

'Hi,' he replies plainly, checking the time on his Rolex. His voice is almost unrecognisable.

'How are you! I...I can't believe it is YOU! Where did you disappear!' I bombard my recently re-discovered best friend.

'Doon.'

'Oh...wow!' I say, surprised. He gives me half a smile. *Ohh*...I see one dimple.

'I really wanted to write to you...' I continue, confused about what to say next.

'Then why didn't you...' He bends his face to look directly into my eyes. I don't know why but I feel slightly breathless, '...write to me?'

His brown eyes are distant yet familiar and make me

feel like we're still those Barakhamba kids living on Akbar road and are here at college pretending to be adults.

'I...I didn't have your new address. I'd asked Dad to get it, but he couldn't find it.' I suddenly feel guilty for not doing more.

'How convenient,' he says in a cryptic tone and starts walking in the other direction. Wait, is he mad at me?

'You could have written to me too, you know!' I say bluntly, unable to comprehend his harshness.

'I had nothing to say to you,' he replies without stopping.

It took me a moment to take in Veer's answer. This is not my best friend. My best friend wasn't a jerk.

I met my school classmate, Aditya, at the college gate today, and even *we* had a fruitful five-minute talk about our lives. Veer, my *best friend*, on the other hand, barely spoke two complete sentences to me.

What's wrong with him?

He knew my address; I stayed right there all this time. He is the one who disappeared! And now he is the one who's acting mad? Besides, it was *his* father who chose to be on the wrong side. Not me.

'Who was that?' My new best friend since higher secondary, Naina Koli, inquires as she joins me in the corridor. She is the most bubbly and thoughtful person I know.

Naina, in fact, is the first person I could genuinely got along with after Veer left. Moreover, her dad isn't a politician. What a relief.

'Umm...just someone I thought I knew...nevermind.' I answer truthfully as we head to the cafeteria before our next class.

Chapter 8

"Back Off Man"

Veer

The next morning, Imran and I are standing in the college parking area, smoking. Soon Abhimanyu and his friends join us, and we begin discussing our first day with them.

Imran mentions the cricket team trials happening next week. Abhimanyu advises us to beware of Professor Mehta and not bunk his classes. He is very strict with his attendance. Sad, seeing that was pretty much the only class I'd thought of bunking frequently. Not because he's a bad professor. The man's a genius. But because who'd like to see Rashika Chaudhary every damn day. Speaking of Rashika, Professor Mehta's class was the only time I saw her yesterday. Not that I was looking for her.

We're talking about the best tea joints around DU's

North campus when everyone's gaze shifts to the white Ambassador stopping at the gate. The backdoor opens. Rashika gets down and walks past us, trying her best to ignore my existence. But not quite. I see the disapproval in her eyes when she watches me smoke. Suit yourself, Rashika Chaudhary. I don't need your approval.

She doesn't acknowledge me, and I sure as hell don't acknowledge her. Maybe she got the hint that I'm not looking for a rekindled friendship or something. *Good.*

'Looks like a *bade baap ki bigdi beti*,' Abhimanyu remarks as she walks inside the main building. I stay silent.

Obviously, these guys do not know anything about my past with her. Imran knows, but I don't think he knows the girl who just passed us was Amar Chaudhary's daughter. It's better that way.

'I don't know about her dad,' Imran says suggestively, gawking at her behind, 'but she sure has a lot of *mal*.'

Imran laughs. The others join in.

And somehow, I lose it. I just do. No one should talk about a girl that way, especially if that girl is Rashika.

'Back off man!' I shove Imran's chest. 'Have some basic respect!'

'C'mon man, relax,' he says, regaining his balance, 'It's just boy talk.'

'You better not say anything about her, Imran!' I threaten, grabbing him by his collar. 'And stay away from her…all of you!' I howl.

'Okay, okay,' Imran agrees. I loosen my grip over his

collar. He straightens it out comically. *Joker.*

'Listen up, guys,' he announces. 'This girl is off-limits. Our Veer Bhai here has a thing for her. *Aaj se ye bhabhi hain apni.*'

'Bullshit.' I roll my eyes as I grab my bag from the Enfield and march towards the building. The guys follow, teasing the word Bhabhi along the way.

Bhabhi. Huh.

The word takes me back to when she and I used to play ghar-ghar. We would have been what…six? I used to pretend to be the husband who comes back home from work, and she pretended to be the wife who got him dinner. Well, also the other way round. Even at six, I realised, Rashika Chaudhary was quite the feminist and smile to myself.

'Men make their own history, but they do not make it as they please. They do not make it under self-selected circumstances, but under already existing circumstances, given and transmitted from the past,' Professor Mehta teaches the concept of Karl Marx's Historical Materialism in our Political Theory class.

'Marxism is not something you read in a textbook and learn. You ought to make sense of it in the world around you,' he remarks, 'Think about how this concept can be applied to our country...let's start simple. Can anyone give me an example of a circumstance transmitted to us from the past and how it affects our ability to make history?'

Rashika's hand is the first to go up. *Obviously.*

'Yes...Miss Chaudhary?'

'Professor, upon independence, India inherited a circumstance of widespread socio-economic inequalities created during the British rule,' she answers confidently, 'As a result, the government of India *had to* choose welfare driven socialist policies...like the ten-point programme, land reforms, the *Garibi Hatao* scheme etc...to decrease this gap between income and opportunity.'

'Excellent! Thank you, Miss Chaudhary,' he praises her '...Mr Singh? Do you have something to add?' Professor questions as I raise my hand in response. Rashika eyes me doubtfully.

'I'd like to disagree with Miss Chaudhary's argument, Professor. The government had a choice. There is *always* a choice.'

'Could you elaborate?'

'India did inherit economic disparities, but the government could have chosen to remove all restrictions imposed during the Raj. They could've let the economy function in a manner where everyone earned profits in proportion to their effort, but instead, they *chose* to impose barriers on the private sector.'

'That choice was only possible if we had a level playing field,' Rashika raises her hand again. 'What about the backward classes? What about the tribals, the scheduled castes?' Rashika counters, 'How can you expect them to compete as equals when these groups are systematically at a disadvantage?'

'I never said the government shouldn't help them. All I am saying is the way to achieve a level playing field was to uplift the poor. Not undermine the rich!' I rebut, 'Breaching trust by abolishing the privy purse, manipulating the fundamental Right to Property, granting favours to public industries, putting ceilings on hard-earned incomes!' I cite examples from Mrs Gandhi's policies, '...helping the poor should not mean expropriating the rich!'

The eyes of the class shuffle between Rashika and me as we argue back and forth.

'There were a lot of benevolent rich people. Nobles and zamindars, who willingly gave up their possessions! For a fair distribution of resources!'

'Not everyone wants to give up ancestral land to earn brownie points with the Congress.' I taunt her zamindar-turned-politician father.

'Some people do it out of the goodness of their heart,' she scoffs.

'Sure. Like the Chaudharys of Uttar Pradesh.' I jest. Students who catch the reference laugh.

'How dare you-'

'Students...' Professor Mehta interjects before Rashika can complete, 'Thank you. You may be seated now.'

'Class, this is the power of the Marx versus Smith debate. It compels you to question existing social and economic structures,' Professor turns to address the others, 'I want you all to take out time and reflect on this rather passionate discussion,' he directs before moving ahead with his lecture.

Rashika stares blankly at the blackboard and is quiet for the rest of the class.

I thought I'd feel better making her feel bad, but I don't. In fact, I feel worse.

Okay, maybe I went a little too far with this. My bad.

Chapter 9

"You Might Wanna Think Twice"

Rashika

I storm out of the class right after it ends and head down the stairs. According to Veer Pratap Singh, everything wrong with the country is my fault. If it were up to him, he'd execute me for the rise in tomato and onion prices.

Who the hell does he think he is?

In my fury, I do not realise when I started searching for the newsroom on the ground floor, making a last-minute decision to attend the fresher's orientation session for The Hindu Daily: one of the foremost student newspapers in India.

Being a reporter has been my goal for as long as I can remember...ever since Veer (ughhh) and I used to listen to the *Akashvani* news bulletin that aired before *Geetmala*, our favourite show. I don't wanna be a news anchor, I wanna be the person digging up the news.

But Dad doesn't know anything about my interest in journalism. If he did, he'd never let me, his *phool si komal gudiya,* be one.

Now now, before you judge him, it's essential to know something about him.

Just like the basic features of the Indian Constitution, there are two basic features of Amar Chaudhary, the dad, that cannot be amended—

One, Dad is overprotective.

He'd never be okay with me covering stories on the ground—exerting myself in the sun and dust, hustling in the crowd, on streets or in conflict zones. He'd be cool with me being, say a professor or a secretary maybe, but a reporter? No way.

Two, Dad is always right.

There is no point in trying to prove him wrong. Amar Chaudhary's wrath is not something you want to experience. Plain and simple.

Having been in the public eye all his life, Dad knows how the world is. So I don't exactly blame him for trying to shield me. He only tries to protect me the best he can.

I finally find the newsroom, the second room on the left corridor. It's an extensive classroom filled with Remington printers and typewriters. On one corner are shelves of files and books. On the other is an oversized desk, which I presume belongs to the prodigy editor, Siddharth Verma. Lucky man, he gets to follow his dream.

This orientation for staff and interested applicants might be the closest I'll ever get to being a journalist.

The room is filled with students sitting at different desks, waiting for Siddharth to start the orientation. But of all the students I'd expect to see there, I find Veer sitting in the fourth row. I never knew him to be interested in journalism. This is new.

He sees me and comes to sit next to me. My heart beats slightly faster. Out of rage, of course.

'What do you want now, Veer?' I ask as rudely as possible.

'Thought I'd find you here,' he says.

'Didn't think I'd find *you* here.'

'Oh I already applied in the early round and got selected,' he says coyly.

There was an early round! Why did *I* not know?

Well even if I did, it wasn't like I would've actually gone behind Dad's back and applied. I'm here just for the journalist experience. As fleeting as it may be.

'Congratulations,' I respond scornfully.

'Did you apply?' he asks. I do not answer. 'What's so funny?' I find him grinning.

'Do you remember that one time…we were at this party, where you started interviewing Gulzarilal Nanda about the Planning Commission right in the middle of dinner...asking questions from the little notebook you carried everywhere...you were so annoying,' he chuckles, recalling, 'God, your Dad was so mad! He decided to send you home…' He pauses, deciding whether to go on, 'And then I threw a whole tantrum that I wanted to go home too, cause I'd get so bored without you.'

I try not to stare at the dimples in his smile.

Of course, I remember. I also remember pestering Prem Uncle to stop at the HMV music shop, putting on the record player at Veer's house and dancing to the latest Shammi Kapoor songs till our parents returned.

I remember it very well. What I don't understand is why he had to bring this up now! It's been five years. He seems to be entertaining himself just fine. He's made it pretty clear that he wants nothing to do with me, and I neither have the time nor the energy to tolerate him.

'I'm sorry, are we supposed to be all friendly and nostalgic now?' He chooses to stay quiet. I continue, 'Oh, you remember how we used to sit together in class, how we used to eat tiffin when ma'am turned towards the board, how we played cricket every day at the park...' I taunt, the sarcasm crystal clear in my tone.

'Oh and do you remember how you forgot all about me, the moment your car drove out of Akbar road. How you knew my god damn address all this time, but never contacted me. Not once!'

My voice is shaking with bottled-up anger.

No answer.

'Yeah, I thought so.' I move my chair to get up. He holds me back, grabbing my wrist.

I try to jerk his hand off without being too aggressive. The last thing I want is for people to start staring at us.

'Rashika...I...' For the first time since his return in my life, he looks remotely like the Veer I once knew. Concerned and confused.

'I what, Veer?' I manage to free my wrist from his grip. 'I've been nothing but nice to you, and you… you walk away in the middle of our conversation...you argue with me...you insult my dad, in front of the entire class...and then you come here expecting me to act like nothing's wrong?!'

'Insult your dad?' he says smugly, 'I thought we were talking about Marx,' he smirks unapologetically...*and the asshole Veer is back*.

You know what, I've had enough of Veer for one day. I go and sit three rows behind him. He knows better than to follow me.

Naina and I head to the cafeteria, reserve a table by keeping our bags on it and then join the long line to order some cold beverages. It's particularly humid today and apparently everyone has decided to switch from tea to Coca-Cola.

It's the start of a new week today. Our first week in Hindu passed in the blink of an eye. I now recognise most of my batchmates. I'm ahead in my syllabus and have interacted with almost all my professors. College has been so good so far. The only thing that bothers me, well, except for Delhi's humidity, is Veer. We have political theory and an english elective together. I can't avoid him forever.

'Imran asked me if you're seeing anyone,' Naina tells

me as we near the counter.

'I'm not,' I reply, intrigued. Why would Imran be interested in what I'm doing...unless.

'That's what I told him. I think maybe he wants to ask you out.'

'Imran? No chance!' I laugh it off. We have nothing in common. Moreover, he's always hanging out with Veer. There's NO way Veer would let his friend date *me.* And even I'm not remotely interested in someone who is *Veer's* friend.

'Or maybe he's asking for someone else...maybe for Veer?' she considers. 'You guys know each other, right? Imran told me you were neighbours.'

Yup, that's what we were, just *neighbours*. I wonder what Veer would have told Imran, and his other friends, about me. Not nice things, I'm sure. Besides, when did Naina become such good friends with Imran?

'Isn't he Vikram Pratap Singh's son? From Congress (O)?' she inquires. I nod. 'You might wanna think twice if Veer does ask you out, you know,' Naina warns as I finally reach the counter and order a cold coffee.

As I wait for my order, I somehow wonder what the new Veer would do to woo a girl. But then quickly force the thought out of my mind. He can do whatever he wants, none of my business.

'That's impossible,' I ridicule, taking the first sip. 'Veer would never do that!'

'What would I never do, huh?' Veer's voice echoes in my ears. *Oh no!*

He's standing right behind me! *Oh God!* How much did he hear?!

I turn around, quivering; bump into him clumsily, and spill the cold coffee all over my shirt.

Trouble!

'Ohh!' Naina takes a step back. Veer looks at me amusingly and starts laughing.

Great, now he's making fun of me.

'You okay?' Naina asks as she pays for her Coca-Cola.

'Yeah.' I place the empty cup on the crowded counter and make my way out of the line.

'Hey...wait...let me help.' Veer follows, still giggling! I give him my *seriously?* glare.

'Okay…at least let me buy you another one,' he offers sincerely.

'No, thanks! I just lost my appetite.'

I give him an artificial smile and then head over to the girl's washroom to clean up.

When I come back to our table, I find a cold coffee placed next to my bag. I pick it up and take a seat next to Naina. There's a sticky note under the glass.

> Your plastic smile is horrible. Try a natural one sometime.

I manage a genuine smile as I roll my eyes.

Trouble.

Chapter 10

"Now You've Lost Us Too"

Veer

Slowly opening the house door with my key, I move very quietly, not to wake Mom and Dad up. It's 11:30 PM. They must be asleep by now. As usual, Imran wanted me to accompany him to the Gymkhana club. And as usual, I didn't need much persuading to go and party.

I know Dad will be furious if he catches me coming in at this time, especially on a college night, but I'm a pro at sneaking into my own house, so that shouldn't be much of a problem. In fact, I've come home a little earlier than my routine time of 2:00 AM. Imran got sick on the dance floor, and I made sure we left before they literally threw me and my puking friend out.

I'm tip-toeing past the drawing-room, my sneakers in my hands when I'm alarmed by the sounds from the living room. I move a few careful steps ahead when I see the light on. Even God can't save my busted ass tonight.

Dad is sitting in his armchair with a glass of whiskey in his hand. His favourite ice box is placed on the side table. He is drinking neat whiskey. No soda, no ice. *Why does he have an ice box then?*

'Is this the time to come home? Don't you have college tomorrow, young man? Or have I taught you nothing?' Dad blasts drunkenly. But I'm not listening to him. My gaze is fixed on Mom. She is sitting on the sofa opposite him, pressing a wet handkerchief against her right cheek.

'Mom, are you okay? Why are you awake?!' Mom does puja at 5:00 in the morning, which makes her an early sleeper. It's weird to see her up this late. 'What happened?' I ask, worried, looking at the handkerchief.

'Nothing *beta*. You must be thirsty, go take *Roohafza* from the fridge…' She tries but fails to smile. *Has she been crying?*

That bloody *Roohafza* can wait. This doesn't look good.

'What's going on?' I question again, moving towards her sofa.

'You stay out of this,' Dad interjects. He does get a little snotty when drunk, but why is he acting so crude? What did I miss?

'I'm not talking to you, Dad…' I reply bluntly as I forcefully snatch the handkerchief from Mom's hand. It has ice wrapped in it, and the cheek under it is blood red. Swollen. I move closer to inspect.

'Is this the way you talk to your father? You asshole!' Dad barks. I ignore him, too taken aback by what I observe.

'Mom...what...happened?' I stammer, pointing my hand towards the mark of four fingers imprinted on her pale cheek. 'Who did this?' I demand, my blood boiling at the most obvious answer 'Dad, did you…did you hurt Mom?!'

My voice is shaking with both fear and fury.

I cannot believe I'm asking this out loud. But I also can't believe what I'm seeing in front of me. I've never seen him behave so...so brutish.

'Dad...did you slap her?'

He clenches his teeth as he takes gulps of the drink left in his glass.

'Veer, I told you to go na, this is between your Dad and me,' Mom pleads.

'No, Mom…not anymore! I need to know.'

She tries to stop me as I flash in Dad's direction. 'Did you slap her! Answer me, damn it!' I roar.

'Yes! YES!' he screams, rising from his armchair. I feel the floor move from under my feet. 'I did! It's no big deal, okay!'

'How...could…' I'm having a hard time forcing words out of my mouth.

'Is it not enough that I spend my day answering the bloody Congress? Now I have to be answerable in my own house!?'

I feel myself losing it.

'How dare you!' I confront him, yelling, 'How dare you raise your hand on *my* mother, on *your* wife! On a *woman*!'

'You better watch your tone when you address me, you little piece of shit! Is this how you'd keep our legacy alive? By questioning your father? Have I taught you nothing?' He slams the glass in his hand on the floor, breaking it into a thousand pieces. Mom shrieks, jumping back.

'Yes…you've taught me nothing. Nothing!' I shout, battling tears.

How can he behave like this! How can *my* dad, my *honest, hardworking* dad, behave like this?!

'It's her. She is the one who's taught me!' I point in Mom's direction.

'Yes her...this...all this is her doing,' Dad turns to Mom, '*Be loyal Vikram! Be a good man Vikram*! What did I get being good, huh? Look at the others...look at that bastard Chaudhary. And then look at me! What do I have left? No cars, no guards, no money or power, no nothing…I'm a nobody! Everything is gone!'

'You had *us* Dad, your family. But now you've lost us too. Congratulations!'

'What did you just say to me? Son of a...'

Within the next minute, the verbal argument escalates into a violent scuffle. I stride towards Dad. He grabs me by both my collars, jerking my upper body. Mom comes in between us, trying to make him let go of me, he pushes Mom aside. I pull him by his kurta, and he strikes my face.

The impact of the slap makes me go numb for a Moment before I hear ringing sounds in my ear and start feeling the stinging sensation on my cheek. I want to hit him back for what he did to Mom. I do. But even as I stare at him with hatred, I cannot bring myself to hit him. How can I? He's my...father. Instead, I push him into the wall, using the strength of both my arms. Before I know it, Mom takes my wrist and is dragging me into her bedroom as Dad regains balance.

'Hit me all you want, you coward! But you dare not touch Mom again! Or else...' I threaten as Mom closes the door behind her.

'Or else what?!' he runs towards the door. Mom hurriedly bolts it, both from top and bottom.

'Open the door! Or else what?' Dad bangs on the door a few times before going away to the other room.

Politics is a dirty game of survival. There are no permanent friends or foes in politics. Here people love the position, not the person. Here, one day you're king, and the very next day, you're the underling.

All this while I saw my dad as a victim. Someone caught up in a cruel power struggle. Someone who'd loved and then lost: his job, his party, and everything that came with it.

Today, I see him as a culprit.

As the night matures, I fall into my mother's lap. The fire in my sleepless eyes is slowly extinguished by my tears.

Chapter 11

"Forgive Me If I Happened To Care"

Rashika

I hover outside the newsroom door with a file in my hand. Inside it is the sample article I wrote after the orientation. Silly of me, I know. I can't do this.

Yes you can. What's the harm in knowing you're good enough?

No, Rashika. You know Dad will never approve!

The voices in my head are kabbadi players taking one step forward and two steps back.

'Oh…I'm sorry...I-' Siddharth almost hits me with the door as he comes out.

'No...no worries, I was just-'

'This for me?' he questions, pointing at the file.

'Umm...yes...but...I don't...' He takes the file out of my hand before I complete my explanation.

'Interesting topic,' he opens the file to the first page

of my article, 'I'll read this. Meanwhile, could you please deliver a message to Veer Pratap Singh?' he asks.

I zone the moment I hear his name.

'He's really tall...curly hair, wears a Rolex,' he describes Veer's appearance, seeing my blank expression.

'Yeah…I know who he is...'

'Perfect...'

Pro-tip for future Rashika: Do not pace in front of the newsroom with a sample article you don't plan on submitting.

'There you are!' I halt, finding Veer batting in the nets, practising for that much-awaited trial match for the freshers' batch.

'I've been looking all over for you!' I lie. I knew exactly where he was.

The funny thing is that even though I had convinced myself that I did not give a rat's ass about what Veer did in college, I'd felt his absence in class these past few days. As much as I hate to admit it, I think I liked stealing glances at him, and then pretending it was only because he was in the way of the blackboard. I liked hearing him answer questions, and failing to look directly at his face when he did. I think I liked ignoring his existence in class and yet wondering if he had noticed me. I felt weird that I could not take his name without feeling a stupid urge to smile. That I wanted Veer to be around everytime Naina and Imran decided to meet in the canteen. That I wanted to adjust my hair when I did see him around me.

'Why?' Veer asks, looking in my direction as he takes his stance to face another ball.

His bulging biceps are visible under his white jersey T-shirt and make him look kinda hot. Back when we were little, he used to ask me to press his upper arm to check if his bicep had gotten any bigger after hanging from the mango tree in the park.

I'm more than ready to press those biceps now too, if he'd like. I feel my cheeks flush, and my palms sweat at the thought. *No, Rashika, you won't do any such thing*. He is an asshole who loathes you, remember?

Veer defends another ball before pausing to turn towards me. I can read the number on the back of his jersey as he turns. 19. Wait a second, that's my birth date! 19 April. But 19 could also stand for his age. Yeah, that sounds more likely.

'You were saying?' he wipes the sweat off his brows before putting his helmet on again. I swallow before telling him the message I'd come to deliver.

'Siddharth wants to assign you some interview pieces. Go and talk to him when you're done.'

'Alright, will do.' His expression is neutral as he turns back and gestures to the bowler to continue bowling.

That's it? No *Thanks for informing, Rashika*. No *How have you been? I haven't seen you since the day you clumsily poured coffee over yourself because of me.*

Sure, no worries. I'm not free to chat either. I need to

get back to the newsroom, take back my article and clear out the misunderstanding with Siddharth.

I turn around to head back when I suddenly hear Veer groan. At once, I look back to see him. He's half bent, his hand pressing against the left side of his helmet. *Oh shit!* The ball must've hit his head!

Without a thought, I run inside the nets, shouting at the bowler to fetch some ice from the cafeteria. I don't understand why these kids bowl bouncers to the head!

'Oh God, how bad is it ?' I ask, horrified as I help him take off his helmet. 'Come here...'

I make him sit on the pitch and kneel next to him. My reflexes make my hand move through his sweaty hair, rubbing his scalp as fast as possible to stimulate blood flow. As I rub and turn his perfectly curly hair into a sparrow's nest, he slowly opens his eyes. I keep rubbing as he places his cute little puppy eyes on me.

But why do I sense sadness, and not just physical pain, behind them?

No matter what I pretend, I realise I do care about him. The thought of him getting injured is enough to make my insides numb.

'It's fine now,' he says after a short while, raising his head.

I notice my other hand has been cupping his face all this time and suddenly feel the touch of his soft stubble tickling my palm.

'Are you okay?' I ask nervously, moving my hands off him.

We're sitting right under the hot summer sun, and to top it, Veer's presence makes me feel like a melting orange ice candy.

'Yeah…thanks!' he responds, adjusting his hair.

'No, I mean, like really...what's wrong, Veer?'

'Nothing-' he mumbles. But he looks worn out.

Something is bothering him. I know it. Despite being a politician's son, he's never been good at lying.

'Veer, I won't talk to you if you lie like this,' I adopt my old trick to make him blurt out the truth.

'And how are you so sure this move would still work on me?' he implores.

'I just am,' I say honestly. I don't know why but I do think that it'd matter to him.

Even though all we do is try to pull each other down, we don't go a day without coming in each other's way.

'Now, spit it out. What happened?' I order.

He studies my face deciding what to say.

'My dad…' He pauses, taking his face in his hands and then lifting it with a deep distraught sigh, 'Turns out...he drank, you know like a lot...and then he…then he...' His words are getting stuck in his throat 'He…he hit Mom…' He draws a trembling breath.

Unintentionally, I lean closer to him. My brain is refusing to process what I just heard.

'Yesterday was the third time this happened...and I only found out last night...that too...accidentally,' he stutters. His voice sounds like he was gonna break down any second '…like I wasn't supposed to be there, you know, and Mom was never going to tell me!'

How can this be! Vikram Uncle used to open the car door for Gayatri Aunty! He is such a gentleman, or he *was* back then. Dad always says a person's character is revealed not while enjoying success but while enduring setbacks. Or maybe that was the facade Vikram Uncle wanted to present to everyone. Everyone knows how most politicians master the art of deception. I mean, even Veer didn't know otherwise until yesterday.

Whatever the reasons be, Gaytri Aunty doesn't deserve to be treated this way. *No one* does.

A hundred thoughts speeding through my mind crash when I feel his exhausted eyes on me. He's waiting for my reaction, but I have no clue what to say.

'Oh Veer…I am so sorry!' I let emotion overtake my better judgement as I lean in to hug him, loosely wrapping my arms around his back, tugging my head in his shoulders. Despite the dismal situation, I feel my whole body electrify as he hesitantly returns the gesture by placing one hand over my shoulder, the other through my hair. Sparks blaze through my bust as I tighten my embrace.

Where there is a spark, there could be a fire. We're volatile, Veer and I. Together, we could be explosive. The thought terrifies me into breaking away from him; he holds on a little longer.

'Do you wanna talk about it?' I ask once he places his hands back on his crossed legs.

'No,' he shakes his head sideways. I cannot hide the

despondency on my face. 'Ahh, there's nothing to talk about, Rashika,' he sighs, conceding, 'It's all my fault...I was the one who went away to Doon, who left Mom alone…' His eyes are reddening. 'I was the one who hung out with Imran almost every night since college started...the one who wasn't home when all this started happening...when Mom needed me!' He wipes a tear rolling down his eye like it was sweat. As he desperately tries to push his tears back in, I gather the courage to slowly place my hand on his knee. 'I was the one who never took Dad's drinking seriously...Mom kept saying it's alright...he's just drinking to cope, that he's just really stressed out, and I bought it. I never nagged him to stop drinking, and look how that turned out…I'm such a pathetic son!' He is distraught.

'Veer, listen to me,' I take his face in my palms, making him look directly at me. 'You are a wonderful son. You couldn't have seen this coming! But now that you do know about this, I am sure you will be there for aunty every step of the way,' I reassure, gently wiping the tears surfacing in his eyes. 'It is not your fault! If anything, it is the circumstance's fault!

'Yes, the *circumstance,*' his voice turns cold as he flinches back from me, 'And who is responsible for the circumstance?'

I say nothing, unable to understand the sudden change in his expressions.

'What do you mean?' I pull back my hands.

'I mean, open your eyes, and look around you

Rashika!' He stands abruptly. I do too.

'Do you really not see all the destruction your father has helped cause? Congress was an eighty-year-old party for God's sake! And they tore it apart, piece by piece,' he accused. 'Your *great* father was my father's *friend*...and he stood there watching this happen, *making* this happen! My father lost everything he'd worked for Rashika... his ministership, his status, his power, everything...a politician is nothing without power. Nothing. And all this would never have happened if Congress would've stayed the way it was, the way it was *supposed* to stay!'

His words are sharper than his jawline and pierce through every pore of my skin.

I knew things had been going downhill for his Dad. Politics is indeed a rollercoaster that keeps going up and down. But I never thought he held my dad responsible for it. I knew we didn't see eye to eye on many things. We were two people who saw the same world around us through different lenses. But I never thought that he resented us, resented *me*. I'd assumed we were two best friends, mad at each other for not staying in contact, that we fought with each other because we were immature teenagers too impatient to talk it out. But he...he thinks my dad deceived...double-crossed...Vikram Uncle?

What does that make me in his eyes, a traitor's daughter?!

'But Veer, that is not what happened-' I try to reason, but he cuts me off.

'You obviously cannot accept your holier than thou

father could do something wrong. I knew it!' he spits.

'You cannot blame my father and the Congress for everything!'

'Really? Then who do you suggest I should blame?'

'As if your dad has done nothing wrong?' I say, 'Did he not shamelessly badmouth my dad on Doordarshan yesterday? Without a shred of evidence!'

'Your dad started it when he blamed the violent protests on Congress (O) in that Illustrated Weekly interview…what about those allegations?' he retorts.

'Why don't you ask your dad if the allegations are true or not?' I cross my arms sharply.

'I will, the day you gather the guts to ask yours!' he jeers with a cocky smirk. 'Oh wait you can't...not when he has your neck tied in a leash like a little bit-'

'Shut up! Just *shut up* Veer!' I retort angrily.

'You can't even ask him if you can join The Daily! Daddy dearest must not even know you wanna be a journalist. You will just be whatever the hell he tells you to be. The good girl that you are!'

How on earth does he know that! And how dare he!

'As a matter of fact I have applied. Siddharth is reading my sample article as we speak…' I snap. *Oh no I shouldn't have said that. How will I back out now?!*

'...not that it's any of your business,' I add quickly.

'Yeah, right...and you can go around sticking your nose into my business whenever you please, right?'

'I asked you because you looked so bloody miserable! Forgive me if I happened to care about you!' My eyes are beginning to glisten with tears. 'You clearly don't deserve it.'

I stomp off the nets. He will not see me cry. He cannot break me that easily. I refuse to give him the satisfaction.

I see the bowler return with a polythene filled with ice. *Finally.*

'There was no ice left at the cafeteria! Had to get it from that *kulfi wala* outside,' he tells me.

I pretend not to hear him. Veer can shove the ice down his raging throat. Maybe that'll cool him down.

I should never have agreed to come and deliver Siddharth's message in the first place. I don't know why I even bothered. Veer has many friends who can deliver his messages, rub his stupid head, lick his feet, do whatever he likes.

I do feel sorry for Gaytri Aunty, and for Veer too, for what they had to go through. But my self-respect has to be stronger than my feelings.

I am out of here. I have an Editor to convince and a newspaper to join.

In the English class post-lunch, Veer passes a chit to me.

I am sorry.

So am I, Veer.

So am I.

I crush the chit in my hand and toss it right into the dustbin in the left corner of the classroom.

Chapter 12

"Don't Act Like You Know Me"

Veer

Dressed in my cricket whites, I sit next to my teammates in the stands.

Our team is batting at 178/4. We have a target of 290 to chase, with only 18 out of the 60 overs remaining, and our wickets are falling like dominos.

Today's one-day trial match is crucial for me. I was captain of the cricket team at Doon. Now I must make it to the college team. I have to perform today. There is no other option.

It's 243/5. Imran has just started to bat when I see Rashika in the crowd. My eyes follow her as she climbs the bleachers and takes a seat next to Naina, who has been here the past hour to cheer for Imran. A tiny part of me wishes that she'd come here to see me play, to support me; a very tiny part that I shove aside as a wicket goes down and I'm called in.

She must hate me for how I acted out in the nets. She was only kind to me. You should have seen her worried face when she hurriedly rubbed her hand over my head!

And what did I do? I snapped and screamed and almost called her a *bit*-well, female dog.

Way to go Veer.

So yeah, I don't blame her for throwing my sorry in the trash and then refusing to spare me a glance all week.

I don't know man! I started to soften when she wrapped me in her arms. I liked how her tiny head felt against my shoulders, and I started wanting to hold her, and hold her tight. So tight that we could not be torn apart again. And when she wiped my eyes dry, I just wanted to press my face against her palms and cry my heart out to her. But seeking comfort in her felt like I was forgetting and forgiving all that her dad had done, and the thought of forgiving Chaudhary triggered me. And I just spiraled out of control.

I shouldn't have. I should have stayed hidden in her embrace. Far away from all the expectations and disappointments.

I tighten my leg pads, adjust my batting gloves and stretch. I see Naina waving at Imran as I walk towards the pitch and take my place at the striker's end. Neither I nor Rashika wave at each other. But I feel her eyes on me. *Me*, not Imran, who she's supposedly come to cheer for.

We still need 47 out of 6 overs. A senior bowler throws

an off-spin at me. I manage to defend and take a single. Standing at the non-striker's end, my eyes unthinkingly fall on Rashika.

My stomach churns when I find her busy reading the book on her lap. She's not even remotely interested in watching me play. I shift my attention back to the field as the bowler starts his run-up.

> Dear God,
> If I've done any good karma in my entire life, please help me score and win this! Let me show this girl what she's missing out on.
>
> Sincerely,
> VPS

280/6. Imran tries to hit, and there is tension among the crowd. 10 runs, 3 balls. This is gonna be hard. We take a run and I am on the striking end again. The fast bowler balls a good length ball. I hit a cover drive. Four runs. Hope sparks in the crowd supporting us.

1 ball, 5 runs. All eyes are on me. All, except the one whose attention I crave the most. I jerk my head, shaking away my distraction. My heart is beating fast in my ears. I have to do this!

The bowler takes a longer run-up trying to intimidate me before throwing a yorker. I step out of the crease and hit a six, winning the match in style.

My teammates dart onto the field and surround me.

Imran and Abhi pick me on their shoulders as everyone in the crowd cheers. Lifted in the air, I search for Rashika on the bleachers. I see Naina clapping and hooting with the other girls. Rashika is sitting right next to her, STILL holding that book. *Great.*

The only girl whose validation I seek the most is engrossed in her assigned reading as if it were an erotic novel.

'Sorry for your loss.' I jog to her as she walks out of the ground behind Naina and Imran.

'Excuse me?' she says, her book closed, but still in her hands.

'The match...your team lost, right?' I pant.

'But I did not support any team,' she replies, staring down at her book, avoiding looking directly at me.

I swear to God, if she looks at that book one more time, I'm going to throw it away.

'Really?' I tease.

'Yeah...I just came to hang out with Naina after class. I'm not interested in cricket.'

This girl really knows how to get on my nerves. But the thing is, I'm not sure if I want to get her off them.

'Really? But you used to love batting with me…we used to play for hours!'

There's no better running between the wickets partnership I know of than twelve-year-old Rashika and Veer playing at the Akbar road park.

'That was a long time ago,' her voice grows harsh. 'I'm not the same girl anymore...so do us both a favour and don't act like you know me.'

Her words feel like blades down my chest.

'Then let me...' I bend closer to her '...know you again.'

There is a plea in my voice that even I don't understand.

'Alright,' she leans away from me, 'My favourite colour is red. I like eating raw mangoes. I hate Maths. I cannot sleep on the left side of the bed. I'm the newest reporter at The Hindu Daily,' she blabbers. I'm taken aback by her moistening eyes. 'There you go Veer. You know me now,' she says, fighting them.

Rashika sounds more hurt than mean. And I feel responsible for the ache in her voice.

'Rashika…' I try to stop her this time. But she is not in the mood to listen.

She was hurt. Not just about our banter at college or what happened at the nets. Her eyes reflect the hurt piled up for the past five years.

I hurt her. For things she had no control over.

My heart is drowning in guilt, and no lifeboat can save it. She doesn't want to know me anymore. And I want nothing more now, but to know her again.

Chapter 13

'We're Only Following Tradition'

Rashika

'Thank you for all your hard work, now let me reward you by assigning you other people's work' is editor logic 101.

The guy who was supposed to write about the Virgin Tree Pooja entered a last-minute debating competition. So here I am covering my first story—a hundred horny boys praying to a V-shaped tree to help them lose their virginity.

But I can't complain. Siddharth didn't just select me for The Daily, he was generous enough to allow the articles I'd write to be published anonymously.

Joining The Daily might have come as a knee jerk reaction to Veer, but now that I have the chance to fulfil my journalist passions, I cannot fail.

I have no choice but to hide my involvement from

Mom and Dad, and as long as I'm careful about it, there should be no reason for them to be suspicious.

Let's just pray I don't live to regret this heat of the moment decision.

Anyways, now that Siddharth has talked me into reporting this annual perverted puja, I'll make sure to provide a solid female perspective to my readers.

Oh Lord...are those colourful plastic-y wrappers... What I think they are...*Oh Lord*...I stop dead in motion when the infamous V-tree comes into view. In the middle of the tree is a poster of Praveen Babi, and hanging from the branches are...oh, well.

Overcoming my uneasiness, I put on a professional face and find some residents of the boy's hostel to interview. At first, they are reluctant to answer a girl, but I play the 'You'll be featured in the Daily' card and get them talking about how they vote on a Bollywood actress as their '*damdami mata*,' how Mr Fresher dresses up as a priest to perform the *aarti*, and how participants in the past years have ended up finding 'sexy' girlfriends within six months.

Nothing they tell me matches the disgust I feel while hearing the actual *aarti*. My goodness!

A few minutes into the puja, my note-taking hand becomes shaky as I spot Veer and Imran heading over. Why is he here? Does he also wanna pray for a *sexy* girlfriend now?

Imran jumps straight into the crowd and joins them in chanting the *mantras*. Veer doesn't join. Maybe he already has a sexy girlfriend. Huh. I try to focus back at taking notes.

I see Veer watching the puja silently from a distance for a while before treading in my direction.

Ufff.

He doesn't say anything to me as he scoots with the guys sitting at the bench nearest to me for the rest of the ceremony.

The puja ends, and I am just ready to leave when I overhear a group of guys standing in a circle. They're naming girls in their class who'd fit the '36-24-36' inches qualification, and debating on which of them has the perfect boobs, the perfect ass, waist, lips. I might puke.

This is locker room talk at its finest and I know I shouldn't be getting into it, but I cannot help myself. How can they objectify girls, girls they talk to and share classes with every day like this!

'Hi,' I barge in, 'I was just wondering if it has ever crossed your mind how problematic this puja of yours is?'

'Excuse me?' one of them says. I'm not sure if he is more confused by what I said or by a girl joining their conversation.

'We're only following tradition,' another one of them adds smugly.

'You mean a tradition where a bunch of boys sit and comment on a woman's body and then pick the most perfect body to hang on a tree?' I criticize, as Veer joins the circle.

'Do you not see the amount of pressure us girls feel

when you put women of a particular size…skin tone… on a pedestal! You-'

I'd expected him to stop me, tell me to shut my mouth and go. But instead, he stops the guys who try talking over me.

'She is speaking, Rakesh,' he grunts. I know he'll get slack for siding with me on this, but he still does.

'…you pray for a girl with a perfect figure, and you get a girl with a perfect figure. Is that all you want in life?' I go on.

'Why are you getting worked up! It's a joke. Laugh about it!'

'Yes, it is a joke,' I let out a sarcastic chuckle '...for male pleasure, a joke that makes women on campus uncomfortable.' I point, 'Look around you, how many girls do you see here? Four, five? This is no safe space...so forgive me if I feel outnumbered and want to leave before you all start discussing what size *I* am!'

I stomp away as the cocky players look at each other dumbfounded.

Chapter 14

"Got Nothing Better To Do?"

Veer

Everyone is out for lunch break. Rashika and I are the only people left in the newspaper room.

She is sitting on the desk opposite mine, scribbling away on her notepad. I think she's probably working on her opinion editorial about yesterday's Virgin Tree ceremony. I bet she has quite a lot to say. She was great out there. Sid had assigned her the task of reporting the ceremony. All she was supposed to do was attend, observe and take notes, just like any other reporter would. But I'm sure she couldn't stand the shallowness of the whole thing. She is her father's daughter, after all. The gene of public rhetoric runs deep in her blood.

I stretch my arms above my head, letting out a phony yawn. Typing my interview with the ABVP president on the growing importance of student activism, took me two whole hours.

It is exhaustingly humid inside, and I'm starving. Packing my stuff, I decide to go to Rajan tea stall for a lemon banta and a smoke. But seeing that Rashika was not done with her work yet, I end up staying right on my desk, pretending to work.

As I type gibberish on the typewriter, I can hear her breathing heavily. Is she okay? Peeking over the white paper loaded in the typewriter, I keep stealing quick glances at Rashika. She still has that habit of biting her pencil while thinking. Cute.

Looking at her sometimes reminds me of a time when I was happy. *Genuinely* happy. The time when I still lived next door to her. If it were up to thirteen-year-old Veer, he would have hidden inside Rashika's cupboard till the time Mom and Dad gave up. But even in my childish fantasy, I knew, even if I would've managed to stay hidden inside the cupboard, Chaudhary would have thrown me out. Just like he'd throw me out when he discovers I'm looking for a way to enter his daughter's heart.

Heart, not pants. *Okay.* Pants too.

But heart first.

I feel my cheeks flush at the same time I see Rashika looking back at me. Perfect timing. *Shit.*

She gets up and walks toward my desk. There is an unusual arrogance in her walk. A pretentious one. She is anything but arrogant. She might be the only politician kid I've met without that typical air of superiority. She could be arrogant if she wanted to. Her father basically runs the economy. But no, she is humble and kind. That's one of the things I love about her. No. *Not* love. *Admire* about her. She is her own person. She doesn't dwell on her father's glory.

'I need the typewriter. How long are you going to take?' She says plainly, taking a seat on the desk next to me. Something tells me she is still mad. Okay...she has the right to be.

There are only two typewriters in the newsroom—one for the reporters and the other one reserved for Sid. For the first time, I'm happy that typewriters are costly.

'I'm almost done,' I lie, unloading my page of gibberish before she sees it. I was done twenty minutes ago. 'I can wait while you type yours, and then I'll finish mine.' I pass her the typewriter.

'You got nothing better to do with your time?' she asks, loading a fresh sheet into the typewriter.

I'd rather spend time with her doing nothing than doing something with anyone else.

'Nope.' I smile as she begins typing. Wow, she types fast.

Rashika

Veer kept sitting at his desk as I punch in the letters. His eyes are glued on me, and I can feel my body becoming tense. I can hear my uneven breathing. God, how will I concentrate like this?

No one comes in the way of me and my work. Why should I not work just because he is here; looking at me the way a child looks at cotton candy? But then again, maybe, just maybe I am enjoying having his attention.

He may have the whole day to lurk around freely, but I must finish this and get back home on time. Dad might get suspicious if he finds I reached home late.

So keep looking, Veer. I'm not saying another word to you unless completely necessary. I continue typing quietly.

I remember Veer always peeking out of the classroom window, least interested in what was being taught inside. Seeing him doing so well for himself at college, kind of makes me proud. Cricket team. Political reporting. A talented young man. Veer's father is a talented man too. I just hope Veer makes better choices than him.

In fact, it was good to see him working seriously this whole while. Although it appears that Veer's time for working seriously today has elapsed. Now, he's either just passing time till Imran's classes end, or this is another one of his plans to annoy me. And you know what, it is working.

I have made four typing errors this far. No correction fluid will be left for the next person by the time I finish typing the entire thing. Siddharth is surely going to burst out laughing, seeing patches every two sentences.

Veer's presence is making me nervous. Can he go and do something, *anything* else?

I've only managed to reach the third paragraph when Imran comes into the room calling for him. *Thank God*. My muscles ease as he swings his bag around his broad shoulders and gets going.

'Rashika Chaudhary, you will be a great journalist one day. I am sure of it,' he says with a dimpled smile before leaving, and my insides melt like a marshmallow.

No one has ever said that to me before. Because no one knows. I've never told anyone that The Daily or journalism is not just an extracurricular to me. It is the one career I want more than anything else. I haven't told Veer either. But somehow, he just happens to know.

Chapter 15

"Just Trust Me, Okay?"

Veer

Professor Mehta is checking our term papers in class. Most of the seats are empty. He has dismissed the class for today, which isn't a surprise. Students are out contributing to the team effort that's a hallmark of the success of Mecca. Abhi and our other seniors have been boasting about how Mecca—Delhi University's 'largest college fest'—is Hindu's 'event of the year', and how our college life is incomplete until we've been a part of this massive college fest.

Preparations for tonight's opening ceremony are in full swing—bhaiyas hanging banners and decorations, societies preparing their stalls and performances, the organisation committee making rounds and running checks for a week full of entertainment and fun. A week celebrating the fervour of youth.

Despite Imran wanting me at the stalls, I had ventured to go to the class, wanting to see Rashika. But she was not there.

Luckily, I run into Naina hurrying down the stairs with buntings in her hand. She guides me to the college auditorium.

Inside, I find Rashika sitting in one of the back rows and observing the dance society students practising on stage.

'What are you doing?' I ask, puzzled, taking the seat next to her. Already annoyed with me being her co-reporter for this article, she rolls her eyes at my presence.

'I'm completing my work before leaving,' she looks up from the notepad. 'I'm not attending the opening.'

'But why?' I ask agonisingly, my voice harsher than I intended.

The only reason I'd taken up this assignment of reporting the performances at the opening tonight was to be around Rashika. Sid had questioned my sudden interest in *Giddha* with his judgy little eyes when I'd bugged him to assign me as Rashika's partner for this article.

I'm not interested in *Giddha*, brother. I am interested in the girl you've assigned to cover it. Only she is not interested in having me anywhere near her.

'I'd thought we'd go together, you know, take notes on the spot,' I try to convince her.

'I can't, Veer. The performances are in the evening.' She starts scribbling again. 'I can't stay back after college...I'm not allowed to, and the more time I spend in college after classes, the more questions Dad will ask! You know how Dad is!'

Oh yeah. I know. Very well.

Old Chaudhary should know better to trust his daughter's judgment and let her make her own decisions!

'But then...how will I…I can't work without your brainy cultural insight!' I respond.

Rashika is the most dedicated reporter of the cultural department. I bet this reasoning will work.

'What else do you think I'm doing here?' she frowns. 'I'll hand over my notes to you when I'm done. You can go see the performance, make yours, and then tomorrow we'll compile them.'

'Rashika, listen to me…it's important for us to work on this together,' I give it one last try. 'Make up some excuse, no! Say you want to see your friends perform or you have work in the library...anything that'll let you come!'

'You don't get it, do you? It doesn't work like that!' she sounds pissed off, 'Dad doesn't know about all this, about the newspaper, about my ambition, or about *you* being in Hindu! He already has enough on his plate. I can't just drop another sabzi in it!'

'Okay, okay. Do what you think is right.'

'I won't lie to him if he asks me, but I also won't spill raita all over my dream by telling him, or worse, by getting caught!'

Sabzi? Raita? Is Rashika hungry or what?

'Fine.' I agree. 'Meet me in the newsroom tomorrow during lunch. We can match our notes then.'

Now that Sid knows how utterly *passionate* I am about the culture and societies of Hindu College, I'm sure I can get more opportunities; ones Rashika wouldn't *chicken* out of. Besides, no point fighting with an angry-hungry person.

I hand a guy passing us, a two-rupee note to get us two patties from the cafeteria and then follow Rashika to the stage where she interviews members of the dance society.

The morning after the opening ceremony, Rashika and I meet in the newsroom to exchange notes. The fest events last evening were fabulous. Obviously, all DU colleges were there! Hooting, cheering and dancing along! It was insane! I'm surprised at the number of insights I noted, and I am actually eager to show her just how seriously I took our work.

But I am more eager for another thing.

I have a plan. I just need to convince her.

'Have you ever bunked school?' I hold myself till we finish typing out our final draft.

'No. Why?'

'You're going to bunk college tomorrow, and the day after. With me.'

'No way!' She rolls her eyes.

'C'mon, I'll take you. We'll do whatever you want... go wherever you want...and be back in college by the last period. It'll be fun, what say?'

'And why would I wanna go anywhere with you?' She lets out a rude scoff. *Ouch.*

'Look, I know you've been mad at me. I totally deserve it, and I'm sorry for snapping at you, I...I shouldn't have. Let me make it up to you, please!' I need her to believe me. 'We were friends, Rashika...best friends...do you not think we both owe each other a fresh start? Now that we're here. In the same college...the same class? We could spend time together, talk, catch up. This could be good!'

'I'd like that too...Veer', she admits hesitantly, '...but I can't...I- can't just bunk.'

'It's fest week. You'll hardly miss any classes. Everyone is so busy preparing for the evening events...no one's gonna notice!'

'But...'

'Rashika, I do not know what the deal with your dad is, but you're in college now...this time, these days, they're not coming back. So take my advice, and live a little. Without worrying about everyone!' I convince her, 'If not attending the fest events after college, at least come with me during college hours! I'll behave nicely, I promise.'

'Okay. Okay, I'll think about it,' she bites her lip, putting the sling bag across her shoulder.

'Rashika Chaudhary...offer expires by last period,' I call out from behind as she walks to the door '...it's the chance of a lifetime!'

'For you. I know.' She turns her face to smirk at me.

When I see Rashika in our English class, I just wave her hello from my bench, without going over to ask if she's made up her mind. I can't sound as desperate as I feel.

Once the class is over, Rashika stops me in the corridor. She's definitely going to refuse my offer. I was an idiot to think she'd get on board with it.

'What's this?' I inquire as she tears a page from her register and hands it over to me.

'A list, obviously,' she raises her eyebrows, '...of the places I wanna go to…with you.'

'Oh. Wow...so...so you really wanna do this?' I fail to hide the hysterical excitement in my voice as she says yes with a wide smile.

As I read through the list, I can imagine her making multiple 'things to do' lists in between classes.

'What?' she asks as I grin to myself. 'You think it's boring right, I knew it.'

'No…no...not at all! It's just...' I can understand why she'd want to visit most of the places she's listed '...it is perfect.'

It really is.

The next day I wait for Rashika in the parking lot. I've arranged with Abhi to get both of us proxy attendance for two days. I know Rashika would never agree, but I want her to have a full-fledged bunking experience. And what's the fun in bunking if you're gonna be marked absent.

Every minute that passes without Rashika showing up, the doubt of her bailing out grows as a lump in my throat.

What if she got afraid or had second thoughts? What if she decided I wasn't worthy of another shot?

The amount of relief I feel when she finally comes into sight a few minutes later is something I should be concerned about.

She has dropped her usual attire shirt and khaki pants for a white salwar suit with a pink dupatta. *Beautiful.* I make a mental note not to gawk too much as she walks towards me.

'Took you long!' I complain once she reaches me.

'So sorry...Naina had so many questions, she wouldn't let me go!'

'You told her?' I ask. She is right. Someone must know her whereabouts, in case...

'Like you didn't tell Imran and Abhimanyu?' she counters.

'Point.' I agree. 'All set to go?' I ask, handing her the extra helmet I got for her.

'Wait...we're going on this?' she points at my motorcycle.

'Why, you'd expected me to book a helicopter?' I mock. Has she ever even sat on a bike? I guess not.

Nice. Veer. Be nice.

'...I mean...don't worry, it's totally safe, I'll ride carefully,' I quickly amend before she completes her signature eye roll. 'You'll have fun, just trust me, okay?'

'Okay.'

I ask for her sling and place it inside the trunk of the bike. Then I take the sides of her dupatta and tie them behind her back.

'Hold tight,' I gulp as she hesitatingly grabs both my shoulders and sits right behind me. *Concentrate on the road Veer.*

Chapter 16

"Now They Can Fly Together"

Veer

Half an hour and two traffic jams later, we arrive at Delhi 6. Riding through its populous gallis and booming bazaars, it is clear how the ghosts of history still live on to tell a thousand alluring stories about this eternal city.

Dad has campaigned so much here that I know these congested roads by heart. Taking a left from Red Fort onto Netaji Subhash Chandra Road, we reach our destination—Chandni Chowk—the prosperous market of Shahjahanabad, one of the fabled Seven Cities of Delhi.

Common legend is that Emperor Shah Jahan had built Chandni Chowk so that his daughter, Princess Jahanara could step out to buy whatever she wanted.

But that was Shah Jahan.

Emperor Chaudhary would never let his little

princess meander in this maze of thugs and thieves. Which I presume is the very reason his princess was so eager to visit here.

I take a right turn from Chawri Bazar road, crossing the Jama Masjid side to reach Nai Sarak. *Nai* because, unlike the other structures of Chandni Chowk built in the Mughal era, this marketplace was built during the British Raj as the centre of books and stationery at pocket-friendly prices.

From brand new first editions and old pre-used paperbacks; from books on academia and competitive exams to books of leisure and love—you name a book, and you can find it in one of the hundred shops and stalls in this marketplace.

Paving our way into the buzzing market, I make Rashika walk on the inner side of the road. Instinctively, she holds my hand as we amble past students crammed in groups around bundles of books stacked on pavements, past parents and children walking out of bookstores, and reach my favourite book shop:

Farid Book Depot

Now, nothing exquisite or extraordinary about this particular bookshop makes it stand apart from the other similar shops on Nai Sarak. Except for the fact that this is *Farid Miah's* bookshop.

Farid Miah—one of the many Lahoris who had embraced a new trade of selling books here at Nai Sarak.

One of the thousand refugees who sought shelter in their own city during the partition.

Farid Miah—the shopkeeper who would safely keep the latest editions of Ghalib aside for my grandfather, the benevolent MP of Chandni Chowk.

Farid Miah is more than happy to see me back in his *garib khana,* as he calls it. I had recently reintroduced myself to him when I came to buy second-hand syllabus books for college. He assigns the customers he was attending to his two employees and turns his attention to us.

I introduce Rashika to him as my *friend*, and tell her about the part-time bookseller and full-time *shayar* that Farid Miah is. Farid Miah offers us *thanda ya garam* to drink and then inquires about the book genres Rashika had in mind. I remain at the counter as he directs Rashika rightwards to the pile of translated Persian poetry.

Farid Miah asks about Dad's well-being and if I'd like to buy something for him too. I would have picked up the new RK Laxman comic I see displayed on the counter for Dad. But not anymore.

In a thriving market where change is constant, Farid Miah's shop has been exactly the same ever since I first visited as a kid. I cannot help but ask him why he never expanded or renovated his shop as his contemporaries did over the years. Why did he remain in Nai Sarak, in old Delhi, when he had a choice to leave?

'*Dil ki basti bhi shaher Dilli hai. Jo bhi guzra usi ne loota hai,*' he replies in one line. I question no more and change the topic by requesting him to pass over the issue of Sportsweek magazine on the shelf behind him.

I do not know what sorrows he secretly carries in his heavy eyes while reciting this verse of Delhi's incurable romancer Mir Taqui Mir. But I do know the sorrow that springs in mine upon hearing it.

If not for Delhi, the city, I would have never met Rashika. She would have never been the girl next door. And if not for the rule of *Delhi*, the seat of power, I would have never lost her.

Rashika returns with an English translation of Rumi's poems of love. Leaning my head towards her, I look into the book as she flips through the preloved paperback. Pages yellowed by the summer sun, some folds-wrinkles here and there. Highlighted verses with hand notes scribbled on the margins, ink smudged by tea or coffee stains; give this used copy a charm the domesticated copies of the library lack.

As she turns the fragile pages, my eyes fall directly on the ball pen marks left by the previous owner. My stomach twists as we silently read the underlined lines.

> *The minute I heard my first love story,*
> *I started looking for you,*
> *not knowing how blind that was.*
> *Lovers don't finally meet somewhere,*
> *they're in each other all along…*

From Nai Sarak, we head to a relatively *purani* sarak in the heart of Chandni chowk—Dariba Kalan—the age-old hub of jewellers selling all sorts of unparalleled pearls and precious stones. Folklore is that Mughal princesses used to shop here all the time! The princess my Mom is, this used to be one of her favourite shopping streets. Back when we bought (not mortgaged) jewellery.

'You go ahead. I'll wait right here,' I tell the Kohinoor sitting behind me as I halt the bike near the stretch of traditional hand-crafted silver jewellery shops.

'But Veer, you have to come with me,' she insists. 'I need a second opinion before buying!'

'No, you gotta trust your judgment,' I assure her.

The commotion of rickshaw walas shouting '*jagah dena*' as they pull aunties hugging mini bags of Johri Mal jewellers to their chests, makes me hurry the bike onto the pavement, not giving Rashika the time to retort.

Rolling her eyes at me, she walks into the crowded market. A few steps in, she stops and waves, gesturing me to tag along. I shake my head in denial and she shrugs her shoulders before turning around again. I fix my sight on her until she disappears into the *gali*, and then head to the little tobacco shop on the roadside.

It's not like I do not want to shop with her. It'd be fun to watch her bargain with the shopkeepers; *if* she bargains. But no, today, I want to give her the space to explore on her own. To be free from someone telling her where to shop and what to buy. For her to turn where she likes and buy whatever she feels. She is not a child who needs to be protected and followed around. She is eighteen. She can protect herself.

She needs to know how it feels to be independent. Not just within the boundaries of a school or college, but in the real world. And if Chandni Chowk is the place she gets to do that, I am more than happy to wait here. Not to mention the kick I get imagining how Chaudhary would have a total panic attack if he knows his doll is roaming the *dangerous* streets of Chandni Chowk alone.

Rashika comes back after perhaps half an hour, with a small cloth bag in her hand.

'So what did you buy-' I ask.

'Is it so important for you to smoke?' she interjects, questioning judgmentally as I near the end of my second cigarette.

'Yup', I cock my head 'Hey...'

She takes the cigarette from my hand and puts it to her mouth, attempting to take a puff.

'Aahh...uggghh,' she coughs and drops it to the floor. 'Ewww.' She spits as I laugh at the faces she makes.

'I got something for you too,' she says, regaining her breath. 'Close your eyes.'

'What?'

Chandni Chowk is not a place where you stand with your eyes closed.

'Just close them, no!' She is not gonna listen. I oblige.

The hair in my arm rise as she lifts my hand and wraps a strap around my wrist.

'Open them now.'

'A watch! Wow!'

'You like it?' she asks hopefully as I check out the black strap round dial watch.

'Of course! Thank you!'

'I noticed you haven't been wearing yours for a few days...maybe you broke it or something, so use this, until you get that one repaired.'

Oh. She notices me enough to observe an empty wrist. I blush, smiling to myself.

'It's no Rolex, but it does show the correct time.'

'Do I look like a socialist now?' I joke, hiding how her gesture spurred a wave of emotions within me.

'Shut up!' she playfully hits my chest and then checks the time on the watch. 'C'mon, we have so much to cover! We still gotta eat, and I need to be back before college ends.' She pulls me towards the bike.

A Rolex is not an accessory you casually lose, so obviously, she thought I broke it. As a matter of fact, I sold it. Little extra money surely helps pay the bills. Besides, it's not like I'm obsessed with brands. It just helps maintain the facade in college, where I'm the son of a former cabinet minister who is leading protests of non-Congressism, and not of a broke alcoholic politician on the verge of bankruptcy.

But I cannot bring that up, not when we promised each other a fresh start.

Before I know it, Rashika is intrigued by the splendour outside one particular shop.

'Veer, let's see what's going on there,' she suggests.

'It is a *jalebi* shop Rashika,' I inform her, identifying the shop.

'Then we definitely have to go,' she says, tugging at my arm. Such a kid.

'Who eats sweet dish before the actual meal?' I protest.

She simply puts her hands on her hips, giving me the 'this is my trip, remember?' face, and wins.

'You wait here, I'll get it,' Rashika decrees, getting off the bike as I halt it in front of a massive board reading.

Old Famous Jalebi Wala. Since 1884.

'As you say, ma'am,' I grin at her confidence as she makes her way through the tiny congested shop.

I see her having a word with the Babu sitting at the counter and then carefully dipping her hand in her sling to pay the bill. Then she takes out a pen and paper from her bag, writes something down and hands it to the *halwai* who is making *jalebis* in the huge *kadai* outside.

What is she doing?

I stay by my bike, not interfering. Five minutes later—courtesy my new watch—she returns with a paper plate full of *jalebi* in one hand and a small plastic *katori* with *Rabri* in the other.

'Look!' she says excitedly, passing the plate over to me.

'Woah,' I chuckle, amused, when I see what's on the plate.

Veer

She got the halwai to make a Jalebi of my name!

'I am gonna eat you,' she laughs, pouring *Rabri* all over my name. Should I tell her how hot that sounds to me? Nah.

'Wait, I'll get one saying Rashika too!'

'Leave it, Veer, it's so busy in there! I had to tell the *halwai* it's your birthday surprise to convince him, and a little tip, of course!' she winks. 'But I swear to god he will smack you with his *karchi* if you ask him to spell my long name!' she giggles as I savour the sweetness of her laugh, and the *jalebi* that melts in my mouth.

Half an hour alone in Chandni Chowk, and she's already learning the ways of the world. That's my Rashika. *That's Rashika.*

After dessert, we head for lunch. Riding through the narrow streets, we decide to park the bike and tread through the even narrower maze of tight and tiny streets leading to the world-famous Paranthe Wali Gali.

Taking a few lefts and rights, we reach the hundred-year-old original *paratha* shop.

Pandit Gaya Prasad Shiv Charan Paranthe Wale

It amazes me how generation after generation, the men in their family joined the business of frying *paranthas*. Clearly, I'm not the only one born to carry forth a family legacy. What amazes me even more is how they keep their family recipe a guarded secret like some formula for nuclear missiles.

As expected, this sixth-generation shop of *paratha* makers is overflowing with customers during lunch hour. A guy standing at the entry point is repeating the different kinds of *parathas* on the menu with the same zeal my grandmother repeated the thousand names of Vishnu.

'*Aloo parantha, Plain parantha, Paneer parantha, Papad parantha, Methi parantha, Mirch parantha, Mix parantha, Rabri parantha...*' The guy could win a Guinness record in tongue twisters!

The tangled electric wires and closely clamped two-storey shops of the *gali* form a canopy that does not let the glaring afternoon sunlight reach the ground. It's so cramped that there is hardly any space to stand on the street, let alone inside the shop.

We squeeze into a corner outside the shop, waiting for a table to clear in the middle of the bustling bicycles, bikes and people swarming past us from all directions.

I ask Rashika to move to the inner corner of the street and protectively hold my arms around her. But I dare not to touch her. She raises her head to look at me, giving me a gentle smile from the corner of her lips. Her smile is smooth as butter, but I'm the one who's melting.

Amidst the aroma of hot spices, her perfume smells of vanilla. Sweet vanilla and salty sweat. I can feel my face getting red hot as if I were close not to Rashika but the *tawa* on which the *paranthas* are being fried.

If she comes any closer, I'm not sure I'll continue to breathe.

God, I need air, and lots of it.

As we wait, Rashika playfully challenges me to *the* Indian tongue twister, totally apt given where we are.

'*Chandu ke chacha ne Chandu ki chachi ko Chandni Chowk mein chandi ke chamach se chatni chatai.*' She goes first, 'Let's see if you can say it faster than me.'

She speaks it correctly, thrice! Then it's my turn.

I'm halfway through my second attempt, stuttering through my rapid breathing when we spot an about-to-be vacated table in a congested corner. Running to it like monkeys running after bananas, we grab two seats opposite each other.

Looking at the interior of the shop, I bet the West could learn about efficient space management skills from the shopkeepers of Chandni Chowk. Rows of occupied plastic chairs and tables, the billing counter, the cooking area—all crammed in one rectangular room. It is so humid inside that it feels like we're sitting in an equatorial rain forest. Rashika ties her hair in a bun, wiping the sweat off her delicate neck. I open the top button of my shirt, sipping water from a steel glass as I scan the shop for a waiter.

Photographs of eminent personalities enjoying the *zaika* of the *paranthawalas* decorate the wall on our left. My gaze falls on a photo of Pandit Nehru, Vijya Laxmi Pandit, and a young Indira Gandhi eating here. I see both of our fathers, the dynamic duo, Pratap and Chaudhary, standing among the people in the background. I notice Rashika looking at that photo too, but neither of us mention it as the waiter arrives.

Rashika orders the famous *hari mirch paratha*. I go with the regular *aloo paratha*. I insist on her trying *achari kachori* too, and order a plate for both of us.

Halfway through stuffing her mouth with the sizzling hot *paratha* and licking her fingers after every other bite, Rashika starts huffing as the intense green chilly hits her palate. The *genius* drinks water on top to calm her burning tongue and starts huffing even more—her eyes watering as she lets out crisp short breaths.

I offer her the *dahi* in my *katori*. She gulps it in one go and giggles embarrassedly as the spicy sensations subside. I grab some *gur* and *saunf* from the counter for her.

Too full to order another, we exchange our plates. I show off my resistance for spice as she eats my plain *aloo paratha*.

For Rashika Chaudhary, I can give up the last *paratha* on the planet.

It is 3:00 PM already. We ought to hurry to reach college back on time, but we still make one last stop at the Kabutar Market on our way out of Chandni Chowk.

'I want to buy a pair and set them free,' she tells me.

I'd thought she'd say something like that as we crossed the endless rows of cages of all shapes and sizes; cages overfilled with white, grey, brown pigeons fluttering and flapping against them. Rashika isn't one to keep birds locked inside metal cages. She knows a little too well what that'd feel like.

We purchase a pair of white pigeons, ones with their wings intact.

'This one is Veer,' Rashika names the pigeon. I watch intently as she takes it out of the cage and gestures to me to take the other one out.

'...and this one is Rashika,' she points towards the second pigeon as I take it in my hands, its tail feathers tickling my palms '...now they can fly away together!' she raises her arms to the sky.

Opening our palms at the count of three, we let *Veer* and *Rashika* out of our grips, into the sky, and watch as they slowly unfold their ruffled wings and begin to fly higher and higher into the infinite blueness.

If only we were those pigeons: wild and free.

Chapter 17

"Wish He Were There"

Rashika

I decide to meet Veer at Rajan tea stall the next day. I prefer not to enter the campus after Prem Uncle drops me at the gate. What if I run into some classmates and they notice me gone for the entire day?

It will only make it more difficult for Naina to cover for me, and I cannot risk anyone knowing.

When I walk in, Veer is already there, smoking a cigarette which he stubs out upon seeing me. He smiles innocently as we quickly run through our itinerary for the day. The first destination I've chosen is something I know Veer would love.

'Still carry that *chillar* around in your pocket?' he asks, picking two glass bottles of Fanta from the crate.

'Nah, *chillar* won't buy much these days.'

'Good for you, I picked up your old habit,' he grins

endearingly, paying security for the bottles.

Something is brewing in the tea stall; something that isn't tea.

I am slightly more relaxed sitting on Veer's backseat today as we ride towards the National Museum at Janpath. Back in school, Social Sciences was the only period when he wouldn't count the number of birds perching outside the class window. He loved trips to historic sites, and this gigantic museum of red sandstone and circular corridors with five-thousand years of Indian history under one roof was his favourite.

There is a rush at the ticket counter as teachers of a school arrange tickets for their students. I deposit my bag at the counter as Veer buys two tickets and a guidebook.

This isn't the first time we're here. The National Museum was Barakhamba's regular excursion point. Coming back to the same artefacts, arranged in the same rooms and layouts strikes an emotional chord in my mind. History is static. It's us who have changed.

Seeing Veer Pratap Singh in a museum is a joy I want all for myself. To me, Veer is more fascinating than the Maratha armour or the Mughal paintings that fascinate him.

The way he measures the size of Harrapa's dancing girl with his fingers and laughs at just how tiny the world-famous metal sculpture is! The way his eyes brighten up like light bulbs upon seeing the magnificent Nataraja idol. The frown on his brows as he bends to examine coins and inscriptions closely. The alacrity in his voice when he tells me facts and legends he knows about these artefacts.

I wish I could click and record all this on a camera. The only pictures I have of Veer are the ones imprinted and framed inside my heart, and for now, those will have to do.

My lungs start preparing for the Olympic races when he casually places his hand on my back as we exit the museum two hours later.

We see protesters holding JP's Total Revolution posters around India Gate as we ride to Connaught Place for brunch. Once there, Veer parks outside Mohan Singh Place, and we take a flight of stairs up to the Indian Coffee House.

It is still early afternoon on a working day, and the cafe is emptier compared to the peak hours of high tea when Delhi's intellectual and activist circles flock in for discussions.

We take a terrace-facing table for two. Thirsty from our museum excursion, I pick the jug and pour a glass of water for each of us.

Judging by the waiter's expression who comes to hand us the menus, I bet he thinks we are two college kids out on a date.

He's wrong. I am not that lucky.

If it were a date, Veer would have made reservations or brought flowers. He would have pulled the chair out for me. I would have made an extra effort to curl my hair the night before, and he would've been clean-shaved.

But that is not us. We are Veer and Rashika. Two people who've seen each other look like aliens drenched in Holi colours. We've seen each other covered in playground mud, with melted kulfi smeared all over our sweaty faces. There is no room to play pretend when it comes to us.

We might have grown up, and moved apart, but yesterday made me realise that despite the nervousness ringing in my body every time I'm in Veer's radius, I am still comfortable around him. It is paradoxical I know, but being with him makes me anxious yet calm.

Gawking at his angelic face as he looks into the menu, I wonder what Veer Pratap Singh is to me. He is not my best friend. He definitely is not my boyfriend. He is the rickety rusty bridge in between.

I gulp as he raises his head and asks me what I'd like to have. Sunlight through the window makes his hair chocolaty brown.

Damn, I wish it were a date.

We order two cold coffees, followed by the Chef's Special for the day: *Masala Dosas*.

Once the waiter leaves, we begin to talk again. Veer claims I am the world's best company. *For a museum tour.* He predicts Imran would have fallen asleep if he'd taken him to the museum as he narrates a funny incident from their history class.

Though I know it's impossible, I want to know every detail of his life in our limited time alone. I start by asking about his time at Doon.

He keenly tells me anecdotes of his classmates and his cricket team—the prank they once played by hiding the winning team's medals in their lockers. The strict junior-senior relations, the deadly birthday bumps they got in middle school. The time they tried to sneak back alcohol during a tenth-grade field trip but got caught. The senior year when Imran worked his charms on the girls from Welham during every hostel social and inter school competition. I want to ask him if he too worked his charms on those girls but stop myself.

I notice how Doon has changed Veer. How it has made him a better version of himself. More confident. More courageous.

Veer's arms are folded on the table as he speaks. The veins in his forearm are popping out under the sun's exposure. His hands resemble a perfectly sculpted Greek God. For a minute I am so overcome with the urge to feel his hand, to grab his palm and brush my thumb over his fingers, that I lose track of his stories. All I want is to stretch my hand to hold his. I want to. But I don't. This isn't a date, right?

Our order arrives while I'm recalling stories of my relatively boring life at Barakhamba—our batch participating in the Republic Day parade in eighth grade. Mr Chatterjee getting so annoyed with the chatterboxes that he refused to teach our class. Veer's former friends from the school cricket team doing sit-ups outside the principal's office. Me covering for Naina when she bunked school for theatre.

And as I offer Veer a peek into the kaleidoscope of my teen times, I grasp how much I wish he were there with me in all those memories. I can imagine how he would've reacted to DPS losing the sports cup to us, how he would have auditioned to act in the annual day or been the mastermind of the mischievous squad who made the fire alarms go off.

I wonder if he wishes his memories were mine too.

The protestors at India Gate are still there on our second time around Vijay Chowk, but so is the police; with their barricades and batons. More in number now, the protestors are projecting banners calling the President's rule in Gujarat and Bihar a sham. The policemen are watching from a distance as they raise slogans demanding announcement of fresh assembly elections.

What if the police decide to break the protest? What if the protestors fight back?

The notion of the peaceful protest turning violent and out of control scares me. Does Vikram Uncle have anything to do with planning this protest? Does Veer even know what his father has been up to after the drunken incident?

I don't have the guts to ask him. Not after how he completely lost it at the nets the other day.

I hope Veer doesn't bring any of it up.

I want to believe that we can make it past day two without clawing one another's skin out. That maybe, we could still begin from where we left off five years ago.

As Veer quickly rides past Akbar road, his old neighbourhood, I hide my face by ducking the other way lest someone sees us. My inner voice warns that I have perhaps added fuel to the fire by choosing to visit Teen Murti Bhavan next.

Moments of our past play like a motion picture in my head as we enter the gates of the colossal house. Teen Murti Bhawan is not just the former flagstaff house or Nehru memorial and library to us. It is the home of our favourite Chacha Nehru, the sanctum sanctorum of the Congress, and a place where we've made many good memories.

From attending dinners with our parents and racing in the open lawns when it was still the Prime Minister's residence; to tours of the house and family picnics in the back gardens once it turned into a museum—there is no better place to remind us of the bond we'd shared and eventually lost.

The security guard at the ticket counter recognises me and lets us enter without paying. I had last come here three months back as a tour guide for my cousin Ridhima and had felt Veer's absence more than I'd like to admit.

It wasn't just the Teen Murti Bhawan. Our school, Akbar road park, the Congress office, even my own home seemed emptier once Veer left. Growing up, I missed him more than I remembered him.

But he's here now. His presence in these familiar surroundings makes me oddly happy.

The outer hallway where we'd once played hide and

seek comes in sight from the big pillared veranda. Tourists click pictures, and young children in school uniforms follow their teachers in neat lines as we walk through the waiting rooms and sitting areas.

It has been a while since Veer last visited, but he remembers the way around the house. We glide into the photo gallery, showcasing the charismatic first Prime Minister's life in pictures. Veer is uncharacteristically quiet as he reads the context provided under the photos.

Both Veer and I have seen and admired Chacha Nehru from afar on numerous occasions but have only met him once in class four. We were accompanying our parents to a luncheon. He'd shaken hands with us and asked about school.

Quickly looking through the gifts and souvenirs section, we climb to the first floor. We've only just stepped into the corridor leading to Chacha Nehru's office when my eyes pop out of their sockets and my jaw drops to the floor.

Standing only a few meters away from us is a small group of foreigners—ambassadors or government guests, I assume—and explaining to them the significance of the study is Dad.

Chapter 18

"Oh Don't Look At Me Like That"

Veer

'Did you not know your Dad was gonna be here!' I pant, closing the door of the empty ballroom behind me. One good thing about knowing a building: You know your way past the public enclosures and know where to hide when Satan appears out of nowhere.

'Obviously! I don't memorise his schedule every morning,' Rashika replies, running her fingers restlessly through her hair. 'What do we do now?' She ponders, joining me near the window of the ballroom.

Full marks for timing, to both father and daughter.

'We wait in here, till we see them getting into those cars,' I point at the fleet of parked Ambassadors.

Why the hell did we not notice them while walking in!

'You sure? No one will know, right?' she looks at me for reassurance.

Nodding, I move back to recheck the door as she

crosses her legs on the floor, leaning her back against the wall between two windows.

I tighten the bolts and sit beside her, far enough to leave a little space between us but close enough to smell her vanilla perfume.

God, I really need to draw a line with her. Wanting to inhale her scent every time I'm near her is not safe for my heart.

'Funny, no? Our hide and seek game is real this time.'

'We've come full circle,' I chuckle.

'I like it in here, you know,' she sighs, bending her head backwards, 'It is so quiet.'

Fixing my gaze at the crystal chandeliers spiraling down from the arching ceiling, I soak in her words.

Everything is quiet indeed. The tourists, the students, the museum guides—no noise penetrates inside the walls of this vast disused ballroom—none, except the nagging voice in my head that follows me everywhere nowadays.

'Can I ask you something?' I blurt out reluctantly.

'Sure.'

'Do you think my mom should divorce my dad?' I cannot keep it inside anymore.

'Veer, where is this coming from?' She straightens up at once to face me.

'I don't know! It's been eating away at me since that night. Why should she stay with a man who hurt her... was violent with her?' I admit, 'Dad sleeps at the party guesthouse. He hardly comes home during the day, and when he does, he's always in a hurry, and we never speak!

It's been over a month, Rashika. How long can we live like this?'

I let out a defeated sigh, staring at my feet. 'But then again, divorce is not easy...especially for a woman! You know...the way everyone in Delhi would look at Mom? Like it's her fault Dad turned out this way! Don't even get me started on how my Nana Nani would react! She gave her entire life to my dad and me, Rashika. Her entire life! And now...to see her family fall apart...God!' I shake my head vigorously, unable to imagine the possibility. 'Does Dad even deserve to be forgiven? Does he even deserve a second chance? I don't know!'

'What your dad did was wrong, Veer, and you want aunty to be happy. You are right to worry.' Her hand slips over mine. 'But I think it is her decision to make. Not your dad's, not yours, or mine. Hers. And I know you would support her in whatever she decides.' She squeezes my hand, 'And I will support you.'

How does she know exactly what to say and do every time I burst like a cloud?

I lace my fingers with hers and squeeze back firmly. I'd forgotten just how expressive her eyes were. Even when we were little, one look at her eyes and I'd know her mind. Looking into her dazzling black eyes right now, I know she gets me. She always did.

Rashika Chaudhary has the brilliant gift of empathy. It was unfair of me to unload my problems on her. This is her fun day, not my crybaby day.

I suck in a deep breath and rise to my feet with the

intent of lightening the mood. Or that's what I tell my brain.

I wanna hold her. Close.

Right now.

'May I have this dance with you?' I propose, offering her to take my hand.

'What?' she sounds surprised.

'Do you want to dance with me?'

'Here?' she grins.

'Well, this was a ballroom,' I smirk, leaning down, 'C'mon, get up.'

She rolls her eyes as I pull her up and then lead us to the middle of the ballroom.

Shy to take her by the waist, I wrap my arm around her back. She places her hand over my shoulder. It is the lightest weight they carry. I step closer as our hands intertwine. I'm wearing the watch she got me. All my time is hers to waste.

'There is no music,' she remarks and I begin a jolly hum of Frank Valli's *Can't Take My Eyes Off You* and sway slowly. Amused, she follows my lead as we dance to my uneven rhythm.

I spin her around in twirls, lift and swing her back, only to pull her close again. Every time she comes close, my breathing accelerates to another level.

Doon taught me the gentleman's Waltz just fine. But it didn't teach me how to act when the gorgeous girl giggles and grooves in my arms.

'Can I ask you something too?' she speaks in a solemn voice.

I nod, my pulse rising in anticipation.

'Why do you smoke?'

I am uncertain of what to say.

'Because I can't drink.' Not after knowing how it drives a person out of their senses.

'Veer! Be serious.'

'Alright, alright,' I give it a genuine thought before replying, '...because I guess I need something...to dull the pain.'

Rashika appears taken aback. Perhaps that was not an expected answer. She takes a moment before moving her hand from my shoulder to cup my face. I feel like an abandoned puppy who's finally found a new home.

She leans in to kiss my cheek, sending sudden heat waves across my body. If only I could literally melt.

'Does this work?' she blushes.

'Perfectly.' I press my cheek against her palm as she smilingly dips her face into my chest.

I can overcome my addiction to cigarettes, but how do I overcome my growing addiction to her?

Chaudhary and company come out of the parking lot after an hour or so. Thank God he didn't find us! Because if he had, then I don't know about Rashika, but I would've been an excellent steak dinner for his foreign guests.

We watch from the ballroom window as their cars leave and then make our way to Teen Murti's expansive back gardens.

I get massive déjà vu as the endless green acres come into sight.

The times when our families came here with picnic baskets, spread bedsheets under one of these aged trees, and opened tiffins filled with bread-butter-jam! The synthetic tents at those charity exhibitions and museum galas. Dad telling me how one particular 'left' leaning tree was nicknamed the Nehru tree—feels like yesterday.

Hell, I even remember Chaudhary's stories about the British luncheons and delegation meetings that happened here during the Raj. I remember it all.

India and I have both come a long way indeed.

We sit on the freshly cut grass under the shade of a secluded Banyan tree, far from the eyes of visitors.

Rashika opens her sling bag to take out the Fanta. We clink our glass bottles and quaff the cold drink, which by now is warm and fizz-less. Yet with her, it tastes perfect.

'I- I got these for Aunty,' Rashika finishes her Fanta and hands me a tiny potli from the sling. A pair of silver *jhumkas* with dangling little white pearls. 'I thought she'd like having a new pair.'

'Wow...you didn't have to!' I'm overwhelmed. She'd thought of my mother's happiness. I do not know how to respond to such kindness.

'Veer, please, don't be mad.' Despite her sweet gesture, she is scared of how I'd react. 'Tell her *you* got them. Not me.'

'No, no...I'm not mad...it's just...it's the same thought I had!' I smile, putting my hand in my front pocket and taking out another pair of *jhumkas*. 'I got them yesterday while you were shopping. One pair for Mom, and one for you.'

'Oh-' she holds them before her eyes. Sunshine bounces twinkles of silver in her eyes. 'They are beautiful! Thank you,' she says earnestly.

'Let me…' I take the *jhumkas* from her hand, sliding towards her.

Pulling her hair onto one side, she shyly turns around to have her back facing me. I move closer, drawing in the scent of her hair. My fingers tremble as I place my hand on her shoulder and pull her nearer. Her back is so close to my chest; I fear she might sense my thumping heart.

Steadying my hands, I remove the earrings she's wearing, one at a time. Hesitantly, my hand makes its way across her shoulder and up her face. Rashika's eyes are on me as I gently tilt her face to me, my thumb caressing her cheek. Her cheeks are soft as petals under my rough hand. I tug her hair behind her ear and smoothly slide in the *jhumka*. By the time I reach for the other *jhumka*, my hand is working on its own. Gliding over her collarbone, my fingers trace her jawline and slowly slip into her hair. I'm breathing into her neck, as my face glides upwards, my lips almost touching her soft skin. Almost.

'Ve-er...' Rashika coos.

I find my lips lingering too close to hers and immediately pull back. My throat tightens.

'I-I...I'll go throw these...' I get up abruptly, quickly grabbing the empty glass bottles.

'But…don't you have to…return them to the tea stall?' she reminds me in an uneven voice. I pretend not to hear and rush to the dustbins anyways.

God! What was I thinking!

I need to distance myself from her.

When I return moments later, after attempting to regain my senses, I find Rashika lying lazily on the grass. Her arm is covering her face from the stubborn sunlight piercing through the thick branches of the Banyan.

I move to stand between her and the sun, my eyes ogling momentarily on her curves. Her body is an hourglass, and I see time slipping by. We must return to a life where she is Amar Chaudhary's daughter, and I am Vikram Pratap Singh's son.

If only there was a place out there—a secret garden, or perhaps an unknown field where sand stood still. Somewhere we could be just us, just Veer and Rashika. Somewhere we wouldn't have to run or hide from our families and our feelings.

If only.

My shadow falls over her face as she moves aside her arm to look at me. I do not move, keeping my gaze locked with hers.

Damn it. I shouldn't feel this way. I cannot.

'Oh, don't look at me like that,' she turns crimson as I refuse to look away.

'Like what,' I tease. *Don't look at her with those hungry eyes, you idiot.*

'You know-how,' she raises a brow.

Screw not flirting with her.

'I will, once you stop undressing me with your eyes,'

I smirk, sitting next to her.

Straightening up, she rolls her eyes at me. Then she takes both my hands and places them on her lap. Her hands are wrapped in mine. What is she upto? The anticipation makes me shiver.

'Veer, answer honestly,' she speaks seriously.

Okay, this can't be fun.

'Why did you never write to me? Why'd you disappear?'

'Rashika...I-' I do not know what to say.

Why is she asking me this now? She knows the answer is not something that'll make her happy. I want to make her happy!

'I need to know Veer,' she almost pleads and I can't deny her.

'I wrote to you Rashika…several letters.' Her eyes narrow in confusion, 'I just never posted them. I couldn't get myself to. I couldn't let down Dad...write letters to his enemy's house! I was so angry...I couldn't Rashika, not after…' my voice shakes '…you didn't see...what… what…the split…the betrayal…did to him, Rashika… please don't make me go down that road! There's no point...'

'I-I couldn't write because Dad forbade me to. I lied…I'm sorry,' she says, her eyes twinkling with tears this time. 'I had your address all the time. I was...just too afraid. But then when you didn't write either...I thought Dad was right...that you didn't want to hear from me... and maybe he was...'

'I am sorry…I should-'

'It is not your fault, Veer,' she interrupts, 'We tried... we owed it to each other to end this bitterness between us, but it will be our fault if we don't spare each other more heartache,' she sniffles, avoiding eye contact. 'We shouldn't be around each other. We can't really be…friends. I cannot lose you again, and we both know I will.'

She gives me a meek smile that tears an A-shaped hole through my heart—A for Asshole.

She wanted me to write. She'd waited for me to write. And I never did. And now…

'Rashika…' I say after a moment of silence, '...remove those earrings before entering your house.'

'Yeah,' she replies feebly, playing with her fingernails as I withdraw my hands from her lap.

Rashika is right. She and I can never be friends. *Just* friends.

But we also can never be *more* than friends. Don't know why I keep forgetting that.

Chapter 19

"Let's Go"

Rashika

Today is the last day of the fest. Summer break starts tomorrow. Classmates are exchanging phone numbers and addresses. Friends are making promises of meeting up in Connaught Place and Kamla Nagar.

It starts to drizzle as I walk away from the college building towards the ground where the closing concert is taking place. Naina is already there. I'm running late. Dad wasn't very keen on letting me attend college today. Protests against the government are becoming robust by the day. In Bihar, JP has called for a Total Revolution. Akali Dal is leading protests in Punjab. The RSS and Jamaat-e-Islami are said to be organising protesters. The Naxalite influence is gaining speed. Delhi is volatile. Dad says that with increasing numbers, they're having a hard time curbing the protests. And so, it took me longer than

I'd expected to convince him I'll be alert and alright.

I increase my pace as I near the ground. Smelling petrichor permeating through the dry air, I am worried that the rain might play spoilsport with the concert.

When I finally enter the college grounds, I am mesmerised. I have never seen anything like it before. The colours of Hindu College are everywhere. Little triangular flags hang in the air. Red and yellow dupattas with circular mirrors embellish the stalls. Students gather around a massive stage built in the centre. The band on stage is playing, *chura liya hai tumne jo dil ko*...latest Bollywood melodies. Oh I love this already.

I melt into the crowds thronging the dias, looking for familiar faces. Everyone looks so happy, so young. Swaying with the music. Singing along. No one seems to mind a soft summer shower. The music grows louder, pounding in my chest cavity, as I move closer to the stage. I spot some of my classmates. I also see Abhimanyu at a stall with his second-year friends. I keep looking around, trying to find Naina but find Veer, instead. He is only a few feet away. My natural reflex is to turn away and run but my gaze gets stuck on him. Too engrossed in the music, he hasn't noticed me yet. His lips are moving as he hums the lyrics. So gorgeous. Past Veer's silhouette, I see Naina standing with Imran.

I should head over to her. But my feet aren't willing to listen just yet. Instead, I walk towards Veer. I know we'd decided to maintain our distance, but one conversation shouldn't hurt, right? Besides, I won't see him for the next two months, that will give me enough time to move past whatever *this* is. I go and stand next to him, quietly. Too shy to poke him.

Rashika shying away from Veer. Who knew?

It's a while before he notices my presence. He appears surprised to see me there. I give him an awkward smile, and he returns a fuller, confident one. The band plays the next song—*Jaane Tu Ya Jaane Na*. I can hear him sing. His voice is deep and hoarse. I cannot look at his face for more than two seconds without turning red, heat flushing my moist cheeks.

I turn my gaze back to the stage, timidly joining in his humming. Through the following songs, our hands often brush against each other. My skin tingles with goosebumps at the accidental touch. Every. Single. Time. And when our eyes meet in between the songs, all I want is to brush my thumb over the raindrops on his face; to tangle my fingers in his messy, slightly wet curls.

Enough Rashika. Distance, remember?

Unfamiliar, unfriendly, thug-like faces make their way on stage. Some of them are carrying wooden sticks. Others are holding flags: 'Communist Party of India Marxist-Leninist'. Among them are student union leaders of other opposition parties. What is happening?

Most of the students in the crowd look perplexed. Some are still too captivated by the music to notice the sudden change in the vibe. Veer grabs my hand protectively, his grip is strong and tight. I strengthen my hold around his hand, panic creeping into my mind and body.

A muscular, rather frightening young man climbs the stage right in the middle of the song and the band stops playing. The next second, the man fires a gunshot into the air. Fear engulfs me. I press my hands against my ears as the screeching noises from the mics reverberate through the speakers.

I feel Veer instinctively wrapping his arms around me, shielding me from the chaos. I hear slogans being chanted among the hysterical screams. The thugs are breaking stalls, tearing posters and decorations. Students are hurriedly running in different directions.

'We must leave. You're Amar Chaudhary's daughter. You can be a target. Let's go! NOW!'

Veer shouts in my ear as he grabs my arm and runs, giving me no chance to process what he just said.

We run out of the ground, past the building, towards the parking area. The slogans grow faint as we move farther and farther from the protest. Veer kick-starts his Enfield, I hop behind him, and we rush through the main gate and onto the road.

It takes me some minutes to calm myself and gain control. Everything happened so quickly. One moment I was in awe of Veer's charm. And the next, I'm sitting breathlessly in the backseat of his motorbike. He is driving fast towards Akbar road.

It is raining heavily, and we're completely drenched. I'm wearing his helmet. It smells of him. My hair is ALL over my face. His, on the other hand, are perfectly tousled by the wind. *Godly*. My arms are locked tightly around his waist, holding on to him like he is the only thing keeping me from flying away with the storm. *Dramatic*.

My attention then drifts back to what *actually* happened to land us in this situation: Naxalites.

The extremist group of communists whose ruckus in Bengal made CM Ray literally cry over the phone call with Dad. Their ideology is pretty straightforward—Democratic institutes are a sham. My dad and all his colleagues in the government are blood-sucking politicians. And the only way to liberate the poor masses is through revolutionary rebellion.

The protest today must be to send a message in retaliation to the government's crackdown of Naxalite cadres in the Eastern states. The police forces must have reached the campus by now. I just hope no innocent student becomes victim of collateral damage in the violence. Naina. Abhimanyu. Imran. My classmates. I pray they're safe.

Luck (more like Veer) was on my side today. But could I have been a target? Imagining the mere possibility that there were people out there today, people from my university, who would've gone to the extent of hurting me, the daughter of a Congress minister, sends shivers down my spine. I choose not to believe it and lean closer to Veer's back, holding him with all the strength I have left in me.

About halfway through the ride, we spot Prem Uncle in the Ambassador on the other side of the road. He must be heading towards the college after hearing news of the protest.

God, why did I convince Dad to let me go today? Veer managed to save me from the Naxals, but who will save me from Dad's 'I told you so' lecture?

He is going to be furious, and rightfully so. Being defiant never plays in my favour. I just wanted to have a typical college experience, not this.

Why did I have to join the most politically active college in all of Delhi University? On second thought, if I hadn't, I would not have met...*re*-met...Veer. I take back my thoughts.

Seeing Prem Uncle, Veer turns around the bike and races behind the Ambassador. Prem Uncle spots us and stops the car on the roadside.

I quickly get off the bike and hand over my helmet to Veer; he places it on the bike's handle. How does he manage to look so calm? Before I can absorb the reality of having to leave Veer's side to get back home, I find his hand in my hair, stroking my head. Unbothered about Prem Uncle's presence, he slowly takes my face in both his hands and presses his head against mine. My heart is pounding faster than it did at the gunshot.

You know that song, *hum tum ek kamre mein band ho, aur chabi kho jaaye*. I wish that was us right now.

Unwillingly, he takes his hands off me. I mumble a sincere thank you and manage a feeble smile as I walk towards the car.

Chapter 20

"Hello"

Veer

I get off the phone with Imran and then Abhi. They're both alright. Thank God. But I do feel guilty for taking off without them. Though, in my defence, they weren't the ones likely to be abducted and used for political leverage.

I had to get Rashika out of there.

I keep sitting on the edge of the sofa and stare at the landline, dying to make another call. I assume the phone number of 15 Akbar road is still the same. It is a number I remember by heart. Taking in a deep breath, I gather the guts to pick up the receiver and dial. My finger trembles as I rotate the dial for each digit. But I keep going.

Call me finicky, but I need to know that Rashika has reached home safely.

As I enter the final digit, I can hear my heartbeat

in the ear pressed against the speaker. Fifteen seconds… thirty seconds...one minute…

The call finally connects.

'Hello.' A coarse male voice, probably a house help, answers.

I slam the receiver immediately and cut the call. This was a bad idea.

But I can't help myself. I have to hear her voice. I *must* hear her voice.

I wait by the phone for a few minutes and then dial again.

'Hello…Chaudhary residence,' a soft voice, I am confident is Rama Aunty's, answers this time. It is good to hear her voice after so long.

Again, I put down the receiver and wait another few minutes.

Maybe the third time's the charm.

The call connects and is picked right after the first ring. Maybe Rashika figured I was the lunatic calling again and again. Smart girl.

I hear a soft breath from the other end and somehow know it's her.

'It's me,' I say, feeling a sharp flutter in my throat.

'...I know,' she whispers back.

'I...I wanted to make sure you were okay.'

'I am, thanks.' Her voice conveys otherwise.

Silence.

I want to jump into the receiver, land on the other end, right into her arms, and assure her that it'll all be okay. That *we* will be okay.

But will we?

Minutes pass with silence on both ends. We just cling to our receivers and hear each other breathe.

Truth be told, she and I have never really needed words. Words are difficult. Silence is easier.

A sadder silence of a long and lonely summer break awaits us. This is the last time she is hearing from me for the next two months. I cannot risk putting her in a situation where she faces Chaudhary's wrath on my account and I guess she knows that.

Our silence is finally interrupted by Rama Aunty summoning Rashika to the kitchen.

She takes a woeful sigh and ends the call. I hang on to the beeping receiver a few more moments before putting it back in place.

It is not just the phone call that has come to an end.

But how do you end something that was nothing to begin with?

July 1975
Post Summer Break

Chapter 21

"Are You Alright?"

Rashika

The first day back after summer, Hindu College looks precisely the same. The same red building, the same whitewashed walls and towering Ashoka trees. But in reality, everything has changed.

The coming generations of students studying here will be running around these corridors memorising lecture notes about the summer of 1975.

June 1975

The month of chaos.

Economic crises and inflation. Countrywide student protests and worker strikes. Judicial conflicts and opposition parties organising mass agitations against the Prime Minister's leadership—the perfect recipe for an impending democratic disaster.

12 June

The Allahabad High Court declares Indira Madam's election to the Lok Sabha invalid, and the country's political mood turns against the Congress government more than ever before.

25 June

11 AM

The opposition political parties led by Jayaprakash Narayan organise a massive demonstration in Delhi's Ramlila Maidan calling for a nationwide satyagraha threatening to bring the activities of the government to a standstill if Madam doesn't resign.

11 PM

As Prime Minister, Madam declares a threat of internal disturbances to the security of India and recommends the President to invoke Article 352—Imposition of National Emergency.

A proclamation is issued immediately. Federal powers of the state governments are withdrawn. Fundamental Rights are suspended. Freedom of press and protest is banned. Electricity to all the major newspaper offices is disconnected. A large number of leaders and workers of the opposition parties are arrested, bringing the agitation to an abrupt stop.

The Republic of India is under the State of Emergency.

26 June 1976

No newspapers are published, and the whole nation is glued to the All India Radio to hear their Prime Minister justify her decision:

> 'In the name of democracy, it has been sought to negate the very functioning of democracy. Duly elected governments have not been allowed to function; agitations have surcharged the atmosphere, leading to violent incidents. Certain persons have gone to the length of inciting our armed forces to mutiny and our police to rebel. The forces of disintegration are in full play, and communal passions are being aroused, threatening our unity. How can any Government worth the name stand by and allow the country's stability to be imperiled?'

Indira Madam's speech made one fact clear—in these extraordinary conditions, any and all power lies only with her and her ministers.

But with great power comes great responsibility and a truckload of threats. Amar Choudhary, the dad, is more paranoid than secure.

End result—I'm stuck with a brawny bodyguard accompanying me to college. If not for the oh so important task of guarding a teenage girl, my 6'2, 100 kg personal security officer could have won India gold in wrestling. In my defence, it was either having *Pahalwan ji* as my security detail or switching to correspondence courses and saying goodbye to The Daily and seeing Veer every day.

And in times like these, I must see Veer. There was no way I was giving up on the best part of my day.

I haven't spent a day without thinking about him. I want to see him every day with my own eyes and be sure he's alright. Vikram Uncle is a wanted politician now. I can't fathom how Veer must be feeling.

But where the hell is he?

When I enter the classroom, Veer's seat is empty. Professor Mehta is already at the blackboard, ready to begin today's lecture; something about Habeas Corpus. I have no idea. All my attention is focused at the window, expecting Veer to walk in anytime. But he doesn't, and the class gets over.

Before my next class, I meet Naina in the hallway. The bubbliness in her voice tells me she just met Imran.

Naina and Imran have been talking over the phone the entire summer. Almost every other day when I'd call, her landline would be busy, and I'd know Imran's on the other line. God bless their parents' pockets; their phone bill must be gigantic.

'How's Imran doing?' I inquire about him to avoid asking directly about Veer. If you want to find Veer, just find Imran. Simple math.

'Aah he's okay, he's just very concerned about…Veer,' she whispers, nervous talking around Pahalwan ji.

'Did Imran attend class with you?'

'Nope, he went to the ground to play cricket. Veer wanted to blow off some steam.'

'Oh.' I find myself turning to the stairs.

'Rashika...class? Where are you going?'

'I'll be right back. I have to do something…'

Before I realise, I'm sprinting out of the building. And another pair of feet is racing behind me. Oh God, I can't talk to Veer in front of Pahalwan ji. I don't have time to waste. I must see Veer.

So I go ahead with the lamest idea in the textbook. I pretend to feel breathless after hurrying down two flights of stairs and request Pahalwan ji to get me water from the tank.

The moment he leaves, I escape to the ground. The things Veer makes me do!

Upon reaching the nets, I don't recognise any of the guys playing there.

Where did he go now? I circle the ground, near the stands and equipment room.

It was easier for Vasco Da Gama to find India than for me to find Veer on this 25-acre campus.

I trace the path from the ground to the Science Block and finally find Veer on the ground floor corridor, returning from practice with some of his teammates.

'Veer!!' I cannot contain the tempest of emotions that stirs within me. At once, I run to him, grabbing his kitbag from behind. 'Veer…hey! Are you alright!?' I pant as he turns around.

In the two months I did not see him, he looks oddly mature. The unkempt stubble on his face gives him a rugged look I've never witnessed before. The sweat under his eyes is making his dark circles prominent. Either he has been crying a lot, or he hasn't slept well in days, or both.

I don't care if all his friends see me smiling uncontrollably at him. All I care about is that he is here, in front of me. Before he can even reply, I wrap my arms tightly around his shoulders. He gasps, and I feel his breathing quicken against my chest, as I bury my face in his neck. My arms move over his sturdy arms, and lock across his back. But to my sudden surprise, he stays still like a block of ice, refusing to enfold me in the warmth I'd constantly longed for all these weeks. Shivers of embarrassment freeze me when I realise what had just happened. Suddenly I'm aware of all his friends gawking at us, at *me*—the girl who threw herself at him, only to be rejected.

What the hell was I thinking! Jumping on him in the middle of the corridor! In broad daylight! I didn't have to humiliate myself in front of the entire cricket team! I could have joined The Great Indian Circus instead.

'Yes, Rashika, I am alright,' he answers disinterestedly, taking a step away as I loosen my hold over him and pull back. My heart is on the floor, crushed under his shoe.

His friends giggle. I tuck my hair. He adjusts his kitbag, putting a cigarette to his lips without saying a word.

Butterflies in your stomach sound all cute and nice until they make you want to throw up.

Chapter 22

"Damn It"

Veer

One...two...three...four...

I lose count of the number of pieces my fragile heart shatters into when Rashika breaks the hug, her face changing from a magnificent Renaissance sculpture to a lifeless stone statue from the Dark Ages.

Dropping her chin into her neck, she stares down at her feet before stomping away in the opposite direction without a word.

Damn it.

I messed up.

All she wanted was to know how I was. And I literally pushed her away.

Damn it.

'C'mon Veer! You pissed our *bhabhi* off!' Imran teases, high fiving Abhimanyu.

I tell them to shut up, my gaze fixed on Rashika's receding figure.

Everything is so messed up. I have so many things going on in my mind; things I can share with no one, especially not her.

Her appearing in front of me out of nowhere, and then holding me in front of everyone completely threw me off guard. And to be off guard is the LAST thing I can afford at this point.

Dad is underground. In hiding. At least until the Emergency ends, if not longer.

Dad got lucky, well, as lucky as one can get when the police are chasing opposition leaders like hounds' chase after sheep. Most of his colleagues have already been arrested.

Everything on the throttling night of 25th June was so sudden! Whispers about private residences being raided and opposition leaders being rounded up by the police had not reached us.

At 5:15 AM, we were woken by a police search party bursting through the door and barging right into our house. No warrant. No charges. Just five constables frisking through our bedrooms and belongings, ransacking the entire place upside down, with one repetitive question—

'Where is Vikram Pratap Singh?'

Obviously, they did not find Dad or any clue to his whereabouts and left for other houses.

Mom and Dad haven't slept under the same roof for the past two months now. He had been crashing at the party guest house at night. Had he been with Mom in their bedroom, he would have been handcuffed and kicked into the police van within ten seconds.

Before we knew who to contact or what to do, information about Dad going underground was delivered to us by trusted party networks.

By morning, top opposition leaders—JP, Morarji Sahib, Charan Singh, Vajpayee, Advani—were all in police custody. Many others had secretly gone into hiding. The opposition had instantly disappeared from the face of the capital.

Mom was asleep after taking a Xanax when I was forced to go to the RK Puram police station later that afternoon. Dad is among the numero uno targets. Given the control he commands among legions of students and party workers; it was no surprise they pressurised me into disclosing his location. But none of their threats or slaps worked. I didn't say anything. I didn't *know anything.* My father didn't trust me enough with the details.

On my way out of the station, police vans were driving in one after the other. I recognised some of the people stepping out. They were protestors from Delhi University's Student Union. College students like myself—the only protesters in the country today—now under arrest.

I made an excuse to spend that night at Imran's house to prevent Mom from seeing my swollen face. Imran's father, the Nawab too, fled to the Maldives overnight lest he is thrown into jail for criticising the privy purse bill in the past.

He is not wrong to be fearful. Prisons right now are like a grandmothers' jar of pickles—overflowing and airtight. No one knows when the police would come calling for them.

Party's underground networks are gradually going silent as the police is increasingly managing to bust secret meetings.

It has been two and a half weeks since, and I still have no idea where Dad is or how he is doing.

Rashika was right. We could never be...

Ours is no personal rivalry between two families. Ours is a national one.

We must think of our family's reputations. There is no privacy that cannot be penetrated. No secret that can be kept in the civilised world. How will it look if this gets out?

Veer Pratap Singh is fraternising with the girl whose father is hell-bent on throwing his dad in jail. The father is fighting for his survival and the son is busy romancing the daughter of his enemy!

It won't look suitable for Rakshika either. Will it not risk Chaudhary's hold in the party if his daughter is continuously seen with the enemy's son? Will they not begin to question Chaudhary's loyalties every step of the way?

Rashika reaches the turn of the corridor as I fight between my sentiment and sensibility.

Call me naive, but I did see the 1976 General Elections as a potential silver lining in the dark cloud of political rivalry. Elections are the time of miracles when donkeys could become kings, and foes could become family. Congress (O) and (R) could be one.

But not anymore. Not after all the bloodshed. Not after how they treated our leaders like caged chickens. Not after beating and torturing our party workers; seizing their private properties, and making their families beg for help.

No miracle can fix it now.

So what is the point of me hurrying to her and apologising? Of telling her that I am sorry for not giving into the urge to lift her in my arms; for embarrassing her in front of my friends, for being a stupid idiot who thinks too much!

It is not like I expect her to fall back into my arms the moment I utter the word sorry. It is not like we will forget the mistakes of our parents and then walk together to the cafeteria.

Rashika takes the turn and vanishes without looking back. Despite every nerve cell in my body signaling me to go after her, I hold my ground and stay right there.

'Veer! You coming or not?' Abhi tugs my arm. We were going to Rajan tea stall before running into Rashika.

'Yes, yes, let's go...' I let her go and walk out of the building with the boys.

I'm supposed to meet with someone there, but these jerks won't leave me alone. I bet they have some sort of *stick to Veer for moral support* thing going on. But I really need to do this independently, without dragging any of them down with me.

I will have to tell Imran, but only when the time comes.

As soon as we reach the tea stall, I see *him* waving at me. I tell the boys he's a student reporter from St. Stephen's who wants to interview me about my performance in the summer test series of DU.

A well-thought lie is the only way I can ensure that they don't interrupt our conversation.

I take a chair next to him.

He begins updating me on what he has discovered before giving me the file containing information. Carefully, I put it in my backpack, hiding it between my thickest register.

I shake his hand, controlling the satisfaction in my smile and walk back to my friends. They have ordered their usual favourite—bread *pakora* and tea.

The tea is sweeter today, or perhaps I taste the sweetness of long-overdue revenge in my mouth.

Chapter 23

"What The Hell Were You Thinking?"

Rashika

You know those fables in which the antagonist grows a pair of horns over his head, and everyone around constantly stares at him. That is how I feel walking the corridors. I'm not sure if the news of the stupid stunt I pulled with Veer has spread like wildfire, or is it because of Pahalwan ji following me around, but everyone's staring.

I'm not used to this kind of attention. God knows how Dad survives with a zillion people breathing down his neck all the time!

After my second class, I, and Pahalwan ji, of course, move towards the academic block gardens. I wonder why Siddharth has called this out of the blue meeting here instead of the newsroom.

Veer eyes Pahalwan ji and gives me a curious look as he crosses me in the gardens. *Ugh not him too!*

Pahalwan ji stands at the nearby banyan tree as I walk to the big old jackfruit tree where everyone else is standing.

'Good morning, people.' Siddharth climbs the pulpit circling the tree, as we all gather around him, under the shade. 'Sorry for calling you all at such short notice, but we find ourselves in unprecedented circumstances. As you all know, since the imposition of the Emergency, press offices have been shut down, journalists writing against the government are being arrested. Newspapers all over the country have come under government scrutiny...The Daily is no different. Our newsroom too has been sealed until they set up proper censorship apparatus for prior approval of our articles.' Anxious gasps and wide eyes meet his revelation.

'There's no need to worry. As long as we comply with the government's guidelines, lay down on political pieces, and focus more on...say, culture, sports sections...we'd be able to operate just fine,' he assures. The group begins to whisper among themselves, but no one refutes.

Veer is the first one to speak up in a clear and audible voice.

'*Raja bola raat hai, Rani boli raat hai, Mantri bola raat hai, Santri bola raat hai. Yeh subah, subah ki baat hai*!' he quotes Gorakh Panday, the famous protestor from JNU.

'What was that again, Veer?' Siddharth questions, frowning. He looks tired. It must be hard dealing with the University administration to get those government approvals.

'You cannot expect us to report only one side of the

narrative Sid!' Veer puts forth his discontent, 'Our job is to be the eyes and ears of the students. We cannot just pick and choose what to publish or, even worse, hide behind other columns!'

'I agree with you, Veer, but what choice do we have? It's either this or closing The Daily altogether.' Veer jerks his head. Some of the others nod in agreement with Siddharth. 'Think about it. Working on other columns would be a good chance for you too. Your previous piece on culture with Rashika was brilliant.' He praises our article on Mecca's dance events, 'You both could write more of that kind!'

'No thanks, Rashika can have her cultural column. I'll stick to my political column only,' he scowls.

Whatever. As if I am dying to work with him again.

'Come on, Veer, don't be a rebel!' Siddharth tries to reason out.

'If speaking out the truth is rebellion, then yes, I am a rebel!'

'God, someone, please talk some sense into him.'

'You can't smoke in jail, Veer,' a guy jokes from within the group.

'Hah, that is the least I can give up!' Veer laughs it off.

On the second day of Pahalwan ji shadowing me, I decide that I've had enough of Dad's paranoia. This is a college with students like me, not a boxing ring, where someone would come knock me down.

Between classes, I plan to execute my own version of those Bollywood movies where the villain escapes the police by sneaking out the back window of the court bathroom.

Asking Pahalwan ji to wait outside the ladies' restroom, I manage to escape from the stall window and land on the outer side of the Science block.

I'm heading to join Naina at the cafeteria when three guys passing me, suddenly corner me out of nowhere.

'Rashika Chaudhary?' The tallest of them inquires, blocking my way. I have seen them around on campus but do not know their names.

'Yes?'

'You little bitch! Do you have no shame? Walking like you own the damn place,' he barks in my face. 'This is our college, we make the rules here, and you'll do whatever we tell you to.'

'Excuse me? What...what are you saying?'

The three of them encircle me.

'Stop playing dumb,' the second guy barges in, 'Bhai will only say this one time, don't make him repeat himself.'

'Tell your father, if he loves you, he'd free our comrades by the end of today,' the first one demands.

'Your comrades?'

'Yes! Our comrades!' He snaps. 'Students of our union who are rotting in prison while people like you roam freely. Get him to free them, or else...'

'Listen, let's talk it out...we...we can come up with a solution,' I try to figure a way out for myself.

'You have one day,' he threatens, pointing his finger at my neck. 'Or tomorrow we will-'

'Move away from her. NOW!' Veer roars at them, appearing from behind me.

'But...but *bhai*, we were only-' the second guy squeaks as they all step back, their confidence shaking upon seeing Veer sprinting towards them.

'You know who I am?' Veer questions sternly.

'Yes *bhai*.'

'Then you also know who my father is?' They nod in affirmation. 'Perfect.' His fists clench as he strides towards them.

'So you listen carefully, and you remember it when I tell you,' he pulls one of the guys by his shirt. 'This girl right here, Rashika Chaudhary, she is my responsibility, I'll handle her...and this is the first and the last time I see you *anywhere* near her. From now on, you stay far far away from her. You see her walking down the corridor; you turn around. You see her in the canteen; you get going. Tell your entire union to leave her alone, or you'll be dealing with me, and trust me, you do not want to deal with me,' he warns. 'Am I clear?!'

They nod their heads in silence.

'Great. Off you go now!' He turns to me as the three bullies leave. 'You okay? They didn't tou..' He lightly places his hands on my shoulders.

'No.'

'Don't worry. They wouldn't dare to bother you again.' He tucks my hair behind my ear with his other hand.

'I didn't need you to interrupt Veer! I was handling them.' I am still mad about the other day. How can I not be? 'Besides, what do you mean...you'll *handle* me?'

'Forget it,' he dismisses, lifting his hands off my shoulders.

'No! You tell me...what did you mean?'

'Alright!' He says irritated, 'If they think I am the one after you, pressuring you into getting those opposition guys released...they won't interfere. That's the only way they'll leave you alone,' he grunts as I make sense of it. 'Their friends...their classmates are in prison Rashika, they'll do just about anything to get them out, even if involves hurting you to send a message!'

'Oh I- I…Veer,' I stutter. No matter what Dad said, I'd never thought that someone would actually ambush me. But I was wrong.

'What the hell were you thinking!' His face changes colours from annoyance to worried anger.

'What? What did I do? They are the ones who-'

'Don't lie Rashika! I saw you jumping out the washroom window!'

'So now you're keeping a check on me?'

'Oh please, somebody has to!' he crosses his arms. 'Which reminds me, where is that bodyguard of yours?'

My guilty face gives it away as Veer figures out why I'd jumped.

'Oh god, Rashika!' he grabs my arm and pulls me to face him. 'Your dad has attached him to you for this very reason...to avoid these very situations!!'

'Since when did you start taking my dad's side, huh?' I try to jerk off his hand.

'I am not taking anyone's side! All I am saying is it's not safe for you out here! People are angry, Rashika, and it's only gonna get worse. You can't just believe the best in people and ditch your bodyguard like this! You need to be careful!'

'Yeah? You think I cannot fight for myself?' I advance towards him 'And anyways how is my safety your concern exactly?'

'Of course, it is my concern! I can't let you act stupidly and get hurt!' he confesses, advancing closer 'I...I care for you! Very much...I-'

'Really?' I jest. The line between wanting to kiss or punch him is blurred. 'Didn't seem like you *cared* yesterday. Am I wrong?'

He has no rebuttal.

'No answer? Thought so.'

I get out of his grip and dash in the opposite direction for the *second* time in two days.

Walking away from him is becoming like those annoying hobby classes your parents make you attend when you're little—you hate going, but you know you have to.

I see Veer again in English class after the lunch break. I'd not expected him to attend, but it is undoubtedly hard to resist the charms of Shakespeare.

I open my copy of Romeo Juliet to Act 2, Scene 2 as Professor Sharma continues explaining the renowned balcony sequence from where we left in the last class.

'...Juliet is beseeching Romeo to forget about his father and change his Montague name. Or just declare his love for her, and she would leave her Capulet name.'

JULIET:

O Romeo, Romeo! Wherefore art thou Romeo?
Deny thy father and refuse thy name.
Or, if thou wilt not, be but sworn my love,
And I'll no longer be a Capulet.

'....in old Verona, it was the name of your house that determined who you could or could not love. Romeo and Juliet belonged to two opposing houses, the Montague and the Capulet. It is thus their *name* and all the identities and duties that come with it that forbids them from being together,' she simplifies.

Sounds familiar. Old Verona or New Delhi, some things never change.

'...and the only way out, therefore, would be to declare their love and let go of those names.'

Easier said than done, dear Juliet.

I sneak a look at Veer sitting in the adjacent row. He is keenly writing away in his notebook.

I dive back into my book.

JULIET:

'Tis but thy name that is my enemy.
Thou art thyself, though not a Montague.
What's Montague? It is nor hand, nor foot,
Nor arm, nor face, nor any other part
Belonging to a man. O, be some other name!
What's in a name? That which we call a rose
By any other word would smell as sweet.

My partner taps on my shoulder and hands me a chit. Intrigued, I unfold it. Veer's handwriting.

My cheeks flush knowing his eyes are on me as I read it.

My name, dear saint, is hateful to myself
Because it is an enemy to thee.
Had I written it, I would tear the word.

Ahh Romeo!
'Lose your name and gain all of me'

I press the paper against my lips and then tear it to pieces.

Chapter 24

"The Sight Of You Leaves Me Weak"

Rashika

Veer hasn't been in college for the past three days. My eyes, neck, legs *and* patience are exhausted from searching for him in the corridors, peeking inside random classes, and checking the grounds again and again.

Veer is rude, obnoxious and so ungrateful! My fingers aren't enough to count the number of reasons why I shouldn't be bothered about him. But not seeing him around, especially with everything going on with his dad, is driving me crazy and I cannot help it.

On day one, he missed the internal assessment in English class.

On day two, Siddharth was livid because Veer hadn't submitted his article for the weekend issue.

But on day three, something unusual happened. He didn't show up for his match against St. Stephens!

Now, you can expect Veer to not care about tests and falter on deadlines. But Veer never misses a cricket match. I mean *never.* He had a 100-degree fever one time but still played an Akbar road versus Safdarjung road kids match. He'd made a half-century in 34 balls there, I remember.

Besides, Hindu versus Stephens is the Delhi University equivalent of an India versus Pakistan match. Why would he miss it?

Unless something went terribly wrong!

I know this sounds childish, but him missing out on this chance of batting for Hindu is reason enough for me to worry and start snooping around.

Asking Dad if he knows anything about Vikram uncle is not an option. He hardly has the time to talk with me, and is so discreet with everything, there is a rare chance I will overhear anything Veer-related from him.

I doubt Imran would tell me anything if he knows... but he might tell Naina. I devote myself to finding Naina in the crowd of students cheering for Hindu.

'Hey, hey!' I reach her, 'Can you please do me a quick favour?'

'Sure, what's up?'

'Can you try finding out from Imran where Veer is?' I ask, 'Why is he not here playing?'

'Why?' She slyly asks. Naina has never been someone to hide her curiosity.

'Oh nothing much,' I try my best to lie. 'Siddharth has just asked me to take notes for the match. I mean the whereabouts of a missing star player should make for interesting bits.'

'Yeah why not,' she smirks. I know Naina is no fool. I know she must have read into my obsession with everything Veer. I know she knows. I'm just not ready to accept the truth. Whatever that truth is.

Having put Naina on the mission of getting information out of Imran, I go to the college reception to request Veer's landline number from the students' directory. It is so difficult to get stuff done discreetly with Pahalwan ji trailing me like my shadow!

Grabbing a seat by the library window, I restlessly await Naina to return with at least some news of Veer.

I go through the assigned readings of The Republic for my internal assessment of Political Theory tomorrow but find it impossible for Plato to enter and for Veer to get out of my head.

What is taking Naina so long?

'Rashika...there you are!' Naina eventually finds me and takes the empty seat opposite me.

'Did you find out something?' I whisper hopefully.

'Rashika, Veer's Dad got arrested three days back. He is in Tihar jail!'

'WHAT!' I shriek.

The assistant librarian, arranging books in the Oriental studies almirah, turns to shush us.

'Oh God! Oh God!' I lower my pitch, dropping my face into my palms as I shake my head in disbelief.

I thought Vikram Uncle was safe underground. It

wasn't like he was creating any menace now! Then why?

How could God do this to them! Hasn't this family suffered enough?!

'Poor Veer! I hope he is okay!' Naina adds sympathetically.

I *really* hope so too!

The first thing I do reaching home is glue myself to the landline sofa in the living room, waiting for the coast to clear.

When Mom asks me to freshen up and have lunch, I tell her I'm waiting for Naina to call and dictate me an answer for tomorrow's assessment. Meanwhile, I open a register and pretend to read.

Can everybody please hurry with their work and get going! I cannot hold on any longer!

Around 4:00 PM, Mom completes supervising household work for the day and goes to the bedroom for her afternoon nap, which also means it is time for Asha didi and Hari *kaka* to have their tea in the kitchen. Dad isn't home for lunch again today.

No one is around. I can make the call now.

I know it is a suicidal move. Maybe our phone is on the surveillance too. But if there is even a 0.1% chance of Veer answering the phone, then I must make the call and leave the rest to my luck.

'Hello?' It is Gayatri Aunty who answers.

She sounds tired and timid. What agony she must be in!

Even if the government is detaining political prisoners

for all the right reasons, I cannot swallow that Dad is also among the people responsible for her suffering.

If *I* am losing my mind without seeing Veer, how she must feel knowing her husband is in jail! *Oh Lord!*

I wish I could offer a few words of comfort to her. But I can't. I mustn't speak. My God what did I just do? Did I put Dad in jeopardy by calling Vikram Uncle's residence? My God. I put the receiver down in panic, pacing the room restlessly. This was a dangerous idea. What if someone traces the call from Amar Chaudhary's to Vikram Pratap Singh's house? That surely wouldn't be good for Dad. *Oh no.*

I force lunch down my nauseous gullet and spend the rest of my evening studying for tomorrow. Or at least I sit at the study table, tapping my foot against the floor as I *try* to study.

At 8:00 PM, I skip dinner to take a warm shower in a failed attempt to calm my mind and then head to bed early.

Maybe I can get Veer's address tomorrow and ask Prem uncle to take me outside his house after college, or no, after the first-period assessment. I can skip the rest of the day. Maybe I get to see him going in and out of the house, or perhaps he sees me and then we can talk.

Rashika Chaudhary, the stalker. *Brilliant.*

I toss and turn uneasily on my bed with no sign of sleep. My mind is stuck on making an elaborate plan of going outside his house.

First, how do I leave without Pahalwan ji knowing?

I could always enter the library and then climb out the back window. But that won't fool him for the entire day. Eventually, he'd figure I'm not in college and snitch to Dad. I'd have to talk Prem Uncle into tricking him.

Once there, I could wait hidden behind some tree, or stand at a small shop near his house and watch out for him. But should I be roaming the streets like this in a government car? What if someone tries to…the memory of the student union guys' threats haunts me...no...no…

I try to distract myself from the scary scenarios that surface in my mind by switching on the tape recorder on my nightstand. It still has that Frankie Valli cassette I can't get enough of.

I press play. *Can't Take My Eyes of You* starts playing from where I'd left the last time. Ever since our dance in the ballroom, the song reminds me of Veer.

I lower the volume lest I disturb the rest of the household with my sleepless antics and then lie back with my eyes closed.

♫The sight of you leaves me weak
There are no words left to speak ♫

I try concentrating on the lyrics but fail.

♫ But if you feel like I feel
Please let me know that is real ♫

What if Veer had not been there on the ground...

What if he hadn't made those students back off? What would I have done then?!

♫ I need you baby
To warm a lonely night ♫

I'd like to believe that I could have tackled them myself too by being witty and firm. Like Dad would have.

But I can't say for sure.

♫ Now that I've found you, stay ♫

I hear a sudden loud thud from outside and open my eyes.

Another thud. Quickly, I switch on the lampshade at my bedside.

♫ I wanna hold you so mu-

I turn off the music and listen carefully.

Thud. Thud. Clink. Clink. Thud. As if someone is clinging to the water pipe leading from the ground to the terrace…as if someone is climbing up?

Oh my god.

I jump off the bed, my heart palpitating in my mouth as I imagine the worst.

Is our house under attack? News of rioters attacking houses of those they hold responsible is not new to India. I myself was nearly attacked twice. What if this time they actually succeed!

My face ashens. Dad too has been constantly concerned about our safety. He had doubled the security outside our home the very next day the Emergency was announced.

But what if someone managed to break in? What if they were angry at someone the government had arrested or something the government had done to them?

My mind goes straight to Mom, who must be sleeping in her room, all alone. Dad too. He would be in the drawing-room attending to people like he usually does every night after dinner.

What if multiple people are coming to attack us?

Stones, fireballs, lathis, knives! Who knows what angry assailants might use!

What if they reach Mom and Dad before the security gets here?

My breath comes in shallow bursts from my pounding chest.

This can't be happening!

I hear a knock on the glass of my window.

They're here!

I freeze like a scapegoat awaiting sacrifice. Beads of sweat appear on my forehead, and my lips begin to tremble.

Another knock. *Oh no!*

I must do something before it is too late. Somehow I swallow my fear and tiptoe to the almirah, grabbing my tennis racket without making a sound. I am not dying without a fight.

Slightly moving the curtain with my quivering hand, I raise my racket, preparing to hit with all my strength as I cautiously peep outside the window...

What the actual fu-

Chapter 25

"I Can Fight It No More"

Veer

I used to climb up and down this window all the time! Cause obviously, why use the front door and tell your neighbour's parents you've come over for the entire day when you have a window leading straight into Rashika's room. God bless the architect who decided to place this thick water pipe to the first-floor tank where I could climb it and land exactly where I wanna be.

However, me climbing to knock at her window tonight is different, in three ways precisely.

One, I was sleeker and the pipe was sturdier back then. Now, not only am I completely out of practice, the pipe too doesn't seem to take my weight and begins to shake as I hang onto it with my life in the balance.

Two, no one would mind finding eleven-year-old Veer and Rashika together in a room post-dinner. Now, if Chaudhary as much as senses my presence, he would roast me into a *Shammi Kebab* and serve me as a starter to his socialist friends.

Three, and most importantly, when I sneaked into her room back then, I was sure that she'd open the window to let me in and wouldn't kick me out. Now, not so much.

How do I know if this is still her room and not end up mistakenly hanging outside Mr and Mrs Chaudhary's renovated bedroom? I kind of bribed Prem Uncle. Prem uncle's a sweet guy with a super sweet tooth. I don't know if the way into a man's heart is actually through his stomach or not but bringing Prem Uncle his favourite *Sev Barfi* from Chaina Ram Sindhi sweets surely did secure me the way to Rashika's room. Anyways, I had seen the way he looked at us, on the day of the Naxal Protest. He'd disapproved. But not so much that he'd rat us out to Chaudhary. So I had kind of hoped he'd help out once I assured him of my honourable intentions. C'mon, the guy saw me as a meek teenager with pimples and a squeaky voice. He knew I wouldn't grow up to be the playboy type.

Maintaining my balance between the metal grill and the pipe, I stretch my arm and knock on the windowpane. Once. Twice. Thri-

Rashika draws the curtain. I almost tumble backwards.

Woahhh! What is she doi?-

She's holding a tennis racket up in her hand, ready to smash open the head of whatever thief, thug or spy she presumed was trying to break in. Trust me, if I were really some spy, I would've jumped off and aborted the mission I was on that very moment. No question.

She lowers down the racket once she sees it's me. Phew.

But even as she does, I cannot decipher her expressions. Is she happy to see me? Is she mad? Curious? Stunned? Or is she simply horrified?

I think I might have freaked her out; it's not like she was expecting me.

I cannot help but find comedy in this tragic situation. Look how times have changed, and yet here I am, right outside her window.

Apparently, I'd taken that Romeo and Juliet balcony scene way too seriously. Shakespeare, however, forgot to mention how your hands sweat and burn from gripping the grills, or how your muscles begin to pump and give up as your beloved looks down at you with surprise, too terrified to respond.

Spotting me lose my balance, Rashika quickly opens the window. She gives me her hand, perhaps out of habit, as I pull myself up. With her help, I squeeze my giant self through the now tiny window into her room.

Hurriedly, she walks to the door, peeps through the hallway and then double locks it. Smart girl. Then she goes back to the window, closes it, draws the curtain, and begins to pace around the room.

'Veer! What! Are you okay? What are you doing here!? Where have you been?' She throws questions at me the way a bowling machine throws bouncers at a batsman.

'Did you know how worried sick I was when you didn't come to college!! When I got to know that Uncle…' she pauses, 'got arrested.'

So she knows.

Too exhausted to talk, I choose to duck her bouncers as any smart batsman would. I'm absorbed in examining her familiar room. It looks almost the same: just no more stickers and stuffed toys. The colour of the walls is still baby pink, freshly repainted, of course. Chaudhary sure knows how to treat his daughter like a princess—locked in a tower of luxury.

I recognise some old photo frames on her dressers—the one with the whole Chaudhary clan, one with her grandparents, a few separate ones with her cousins. The usual pictures with siblings are missing. Both Rashika and I are single children. Our parents might even have seen us as long lost siblings. Thankfully the thought of us celebrating Raksha Bandhan never crossed their brilliant minds. If I'm entirely truthful, I kind of always had the hots for Rashika. *Feelings.* I had feelings for Rashika for as long as I can remember. *Yeah okay*. I still have feelings for Rashika. I know. Believe me, I know. For they never really went away, I guess. They were always there, pushed back, beaten down, strangled, starved and locked away in a dark dungeon deep within my heart. But they were still there in my heart.

Maybe that's why I haven't been able to date any girl. I used to make all kinds of excuses—I was still too young to be in love. Doon was an all-boys school. Welham Girls was too far away to maintain a relationship—any excuse to deny the truth.

There are new pictures too—ones I've not seen before. There's one of Rashika and Naina at some cultural dance. Another one of Rashika and a Pomeranian. Aah, she got a dog! I hope I don't bump into it on my way down.

The picture of her with me, the one clicked on my eighth birthday, is missing. It is no longer here among the other pictures decorating her room. She removed it. *Obviously.* What else was I expecting? That my picture was the last thing she saw before going to bed every night and the first thing she saw in the morning? Despite all the practicality behind why she must have removed it, my heart starts to shrink.

I try offering myself false consolation: it was only the picture she removed, and not me, her once best friend, from her life.

The thought of her being with anyone but me feels like being bitten by a rabid dog. And I want to shove fourteen injections into someone who might have touched her...*kissed* her?

'Where the hell did you disappear huh?' Rashika's bowling attack continues in the background. 'And what if someone sees you here!'

In all of her questions, never once did she ask me to leave.

'Veer!! I am asking you something! ANSWER ME!' She commands, moving closer in my direction. I just stand there gawking at her like a moron.

I didn't know how to define it back then. I didn't know why I feel conscious about everything I do around her? And yet why I always wanted to be near her? Why she gets under my skin without even trying to? Why every word out of her mouth, every insult even, gets imprinted in my long-term memory? Why I replay everything she does or says to me in my dreams? Or why she keeps running marathons in my mind when I'm awake?

I didn't understand what starts happening to me every time she's in the same room as me, or even worse, comes closer to me, like she is now.

I didn't know what to call it back then…but now, seeing her standing in front of me, all distressed, panicking, and worried for me, I know what it has been all this time.

I am in love with her.

I have always been in love with her.

My neighbour. My best friend. My arch enemy. My classmate. My everything.

In all roles and at all times, it was her. It has always been her.

At the back of my mind, I think I always knew. But I couldn't admit it, not even to myself.

Loving her feels like betraying the people who love me—my family and all that they stand for. But I can fight it no more.

I want her.

I *need* her. I just do.

It is as simple and as complicated as that.

Rashika is waiting for me to respond and explain myself. But I do not know what to tell her. I don't know why I came here tonight. I'm sober. So it's not like I'm acting under some intoxication. But, surely, I am intoxicated by love. *Oh shut up Veer.*

But if I had to pick a reason—except the invisible magnet that attracts me to her—she's the one who'd understand me without judging or making fun, or thinking me weak for breaking down.

And I wanted to see her. *So bad.*

'Veer,' she almost pleads.

I stay quiet. Perhaps some things are better left unsaid.

'I heard about Uncle's arrest, Veer,' she continues, now standing less than a foot away from me. She has stopped hyperventilating and sounds calmer now, 'How are you?'

My usual answer to anyone – my friends, relatives and party workers – who've asked me this question for the past three days would be 'Fine'—the most useless adverb in the English dictionary, which basically tells you nothing. But I cannot lie to Rashika and tell her I'm *fine*, whatever the hell that word means.

By the time I decide on what to say, her attention has completely shifted to my bruises that have become visible to her under the light of her bedside lamp.

I feel the rigid mask I wear on my face cracking as her eyes travel from my blackened eye to the marks on my upper left cheek and the cut on my lower lip.

'Did you get into a fight?' she asks apprehensively. 'Who did this to you?'

I do not answer.

'The police?' she makes a reluctant guess. I nod, tears shimmering in my eyes.

Her eyes are welling up too. I don't know if it is because she sees I'm hurt, or because she has finally uncovered her father's lies and realises that my injuries are an outcome of the decisions made by her father's government.

She has always considered Chaudhary a symbol of perfection. She could write a whole *prashasti* on why she looks up to him. There was a time I looked up to him too. But that was *long* ago. I know better now.

At this point, I expect her to bombard me with all sorts of questions, like the investigative journalist she is. Why? When? Where? How?

But what she did next completely takes me by surprise.

Slowly, she brings her hand to my face and gently caresses her thumb over my swollen left cheek. It stings, but in the best way possible. I almost let out a sharp gasp as she brings her face closer to me, her eyes moving down to my lips. I can hear her heart beating fast against her chest. Or maybe it is mine.

Rashika isn't your stereotypical pretty girl. She has chubby cheeks, thin lips and a broad forehead. Rashika isn't pretty, not by those stupid standards. She is beautiful. My God, so beautiful. Looking at her face, just inches away from mine takes my breath away, and trust me, I'm already really short of breath. I feel my chest rise and fall rapidly as she reluctantly goes on to touch the fresh wound on my lower lip with her fingers. I wince and she quickly pulls back her hand, but I grab it in mine, kissing her palm with my wounded lips. I flush, sensing a wonderful tightening sensation in my jeans as Rashika takes my face in her hands and kisses the blackened corner of my eye.

Squeezing my eyes shut, I relish the cool wetness of her rosy lips on my burning skin. A tear comes rolling down my closed eyelid. She traces it off with her finger. Our eyes meet as I interlace my fingers with hers. In a moment of dwindling resolve and sudden daring, I lean in to kiss her.

I'd expected a sharp slap across my face the second my aching lips crashed against hers. But I didn't. She didn't pull away from me.

She *didn't* pull away.

Dear God,

Thank you for giving me the present I have asked for since my thirteenth birthday, even if it is six years and eight months late.

Sincerely,

VPS

Chapter 26

"Back Home"

Rashika

I will be lying if I say I'd never fantasised about having Veer in my room or never wondered how his lips would feel moulding into mine; how his tall, muscular frame would move against my tiny body.

But *this*—the agonizing luscious way our lips move in sync as I return his gesture, the urgency with which his mouth devours mine. The way my whole body responds to him as a wild sunflower responds to the blazing hot sun—feels more surreal than I'd ever imagined.

Kissing him feels like coming back home after a long tiring day.

I can feel the cut on his lower lip while we kiss. I can taste the warm salty blood oozing out of it. A vicious part of me wants to bite him, to hurt him, like he hurt me. But I can't. His blood in my mouth feels like him pouring his pain in me, and I'll gladly take it. I'd take it all in if I could.

I can sense him smiling into our kiss as he tangles his hands in my wavy locks and slowly plunges into my neckline. His kiss is gentle yet brutish. Clumsy yet ideal. My belly is overwhelmed with tingling and throbbing sensations; the feelings of all common sense and rationality leaving my body and jumping out the window, as I glide my hands over his arms and shoulders.

My mind unwillingly wanders to think about the lips he's kissed before me. The lips he'll kiss after having tasted mine; if he'd ever kiss anyone with the same passion and hunger again. The mere thought of him being close to a girl who is not me peels my insides like a knife peeling an apple. No, I don't want to think of any other girls. Right now, he belongs to me and me alone. I possessively tug my hands in his hair, bringing his face back up and deepening our kiss. Veer moans into my mouth, making me feel wanted and powerful in a way I never have before.

There is an unspoken understanding between us as I pull him to my bed. I do not want to waste this moment. I *cannot* let him go, not yet. Breathlessly we stare into each other's eyes. Neither of us says a word, but we both know the answer.

His family will never accept me. My family will never accept him. We understand each other too well to know that we will *never* betray our families no matter what. After all that my family has given me—the privilege, the comfort, the opportunity—I cannot betray them. I cannot jeopardise my father's reputation, who's done nothing but protect me all my life. Veer, too, cannot leave his mother alone with his alcoholic father. His father will need help overcoming his addiction and restarting his life. Veer's family needs his support, now more than ever. And I can never ask him to do anything but that.

The sun can never rise in the West. Veer Pratap Singh and Rashika Chaudhary can never be together. These are universal facts we always knew and cannot change.

As he pulls me closer to him, as close as the air between us allows, the thought of someone bursting in and catching us sends shivers through my spine. A voice in my head still begs me to break the kiss, to take my hands off his neck, to stop tangling my fingers through his hair; to push him back and ask him to leave. It urges me to stop with this reckless madness.

But I don't.

I can't.

I may never be this lucky again. I may never feel these firecrackers bursting within me the way they do when Veer climbs on top of me.

I've never been a risk-taker. I've always followed the rules and stayed as far from danger and devilry as possible. But knowing he needs me as badly and desperately as I need him is worth all the risk and rebellion.

Tonight I don't care about getting caught. Tonight, I'm ready to go down in flames.

Inside this closed room, there is no rivalry, no responsibility. No politics.

In here, I am his and he is mine.

And if our first time is also our last. So be it.

Chapter 27

"I Do, Too"

Veer

Most of our life is a series of images passing us like towns on a highway. But sometimes a moment stuns us as it happens. And we know right there that this moment is more than a fleeting image. We know that this moment, every part of it, will live on forever.

I lie flat on my back with Rashika's head resting on my shoulder. Pulling her close, I wrap my arms around her and we lie still. I hold her, and she holds me.

There is a lot to be said. We haven't really talked since I jumped into her room, let alone address the elephant in the room—my father is in jail.

She doesn't ask me anything. I know she wants to, but I also know that she wouldn't pester me into telling her until I'm ready.

I gently tug back a wild lock of wavy hair falling on her eye behind her ear. I can sense her breath rising with my touch, but she doesn't shy away and keeps looking directly at me.

'Does it still hurt?' she finally speaks, brushing her lips over the bruise on my lower neck from when the policeman tried to drag me out by my collar.

'Not anymore,' I smile, looking down at her.

'Who did this to you Veer?' she asks, her voice filled with concern.

I bet she knows the answer.

'When we got news of Dad's arrest, I rushed to Tihar. I had to see him, to make sure he was okay. But they wouldn't let me in...wouldn't disclose any grounds for his arrest, wouldn't let us get him a lawyer. Nothing! They didn't even bother to inform us—his immediate family—of the arrest. We got to know through those networks of party cadres; you know what I mean,' I speak in one go, frustration evident in my tone.

'I tried and tried, again and again, to ask them, *beg* them to let me just see, if not talk to him...but nothing worked...so I went home, and tried out a few connections, a few calls here and there, spent a day personally meeting some people of influence...but no. Everyone is just too scared to get involved...bloody sycophants. Some of those cowards outrightly refused even to see me—the son of the opposition leader without any power or money to offer,' I scoff, jerking my head. 'So then today evening... I again went down to the jail…and insisted that I talk to the head jailer...but the two guards there wouldn't let me. They started pushing me and swore at me, and when I pushed back, they got violent...Imran had to jump in to stop them...and then a constable came and said he'd arrest me too if I show up at the jail premises again. Huh…' I continue, short of breath.

'When I went home, Mom was crying. The husband of one of her friends had died in police custody...and then I returned with a beaten-up face, and without any information about Dad…and she started crying even more...after all that Dad put her through, she still cares about him! And I can't -' my voice fumbles. 'I cannot see her like this! She is sleeping now; I made her *haldi doodh*.' I fail at putting on the littlest smile. 'But tomorrow...I don't know what tomorrow will be like.'

Rashika listens to me but stays quiet. I mean, what can she say? She says nothing and instead just hugs me tighter, squeezing me in her slender arms, and for me, that is more than enough.

'I don't know why but despite all he has done...I-' I find it challenging to put into words. 'I haven't forgiven him…but I feel bad for him...bad that he is going through all this...that he's...well, locked, in some rat-hole of a prison cell, living God knows how! But then again...I feel guilty for worrying about the man who raised his hand on my mother. She might forgive him...but I can't bring myself to forgive him...maybe...maybe he deserves all this.'

'You don't mean that, Veer. That man is your father.

It's natural you feel this way,' she says, and she is right.

I sigh.

'I just want him to be alright,' I say honestly. 'The last time we spoke was that night, the night I found out about the drinking...and he slapped me.' Rashika's face changes colours in shock...*aah right*...Rashika didn't know about the slap. I'd smartly skipped the bit about him striking his 19-year-old son's face. I found it too personal and embarrassing to share at the time. She cutely kisses my cheek, moving her hand over my forehead and hair—her way of saying she was sorry. I try not to get carried away and return to the incident.

'Afterwards, he got so busy with the JP protests. He was either travelling or sleeping at the party office or his colleagues' guest rooms. He was avoiding us, and that was perfectly okay with me...I didn't want him anywhere near Mom when I wasn't around...but then this Emergency happened, and he was so distant from us...he didn't even trust me enough to tell me he was disappearing underground. And now that he's under arrest, I can't even find out how they're treating him! What if he doesn't even want to see me Rashika? What if he loathes me like I loathe him?'

'He doesn't.' She echoes the voice in my heart.

'The way we behaved that night...like bloodthirsty predators grabbing each other's necks...I don't want that to be our last memory together. I want a chance to amend things, to help him get over this addiction, to fix my family if that is still possible at all. He used to be a good man, you know. He was a good-' I choke.

'Hey, look at me,' Rashika takes my face in both her hands. 'You mustn't lose hope. You will get the chance. You will, and you'll be a family again, so strong that nothing will drive you apart. But you must be there for your mother, and when the time comes for your father too...like I'll be there for you.'

I want to say that I'd be there for her too. That she can count on me. But that's not entirely true. I'm the man of the house now. I must do what's best for my mother.

I do trust Chaudhary to protect Rashika. He loves her as much as I do, if not more.

'Aaahh...I hope that is true...but what if I never see him again? What if they hurt him?'

'They won't!' she says positively, and coming from her, I believe it.

She wishes well for her father's rival. Rashika is not her father. Just like I'm not my father. We might have grown up in their shadows and reputations, but we're not our parents.

But I was a jerk to her.

I was so angry at life; I began blaming Rashika too. I taunted her, said hurtful and mean things to her when she had nothing to do with what was happening. I was stupid.

I even made fun of her for having that bodyguard at college. Weird as it sounds I was kind of jealous that some other guy gets to freely follow her around all day when I want to be the one doing that.

'I know all this has not been easy for you either,' I admit. Yes, failure is difficult. But success too is not easy. Chaudhary would hardly have time for his family. I'm sure he would scream and snap at her for petty things. Living in a house crowded by people and their 24x7 scrutiny is not a cakewalk, and the Emergency is no sweet cherry to top it off. Having to doubt your own father's words and intentions, starting to see truth in all the trash people talk about him, messes you up and makes you question your whole Goddamn existence. Take my word for it.

I was so caught up in my own struggles; I forgot to consider hers.

'I'm sorry for the things I said to you. I was just so angry...I didn't mean to be hurtful, or maybe I did...I just wanted someone to blame, I guess, and I took it all out on you. But that was so unfair of me, Rashika. I was wrong. I am sorry!'

I cannot even begin to imagine the constant fear of being attacked or ambushed she has to go through. Hindu is my territory now. No one would dare to lay an eye on her there. But there is a big bad world outside the four walls of college.

'Those student union kids had NO right to threaten or question you like that. They will never do it again, I promise you.' I assure her, 'But you have to promise me Rashika, you won't ditch that bodyguard again, alright? You will be careful and confident and not question yourself or your abilities even for a second. No matter what anyone says!'

She agrees with small nods into my chest.

'You always speak up for what you think is right. You don't dismiss or belittle people who disagree with you. You stand by people you love...' I'm drawn to kiss her head. 'You are a *good* person. You better remember that!'

'I will, thank you.' The moisture in her eyes sparkles as she nods earnestly.

'What?' she implores as I keep watching without saying anything further. I don't know how much more I can say without blurting out those eight letters.

'Everything is so uncertain Rashika...I have no clue what to expect or do next...and I don't know why but I'm also so...so scared for Dad. I'm worried.'

'We worry about the people we love, Veer,' she reassures, still holding me tight.

'Is that why you were...worried about me? Do you…'

I can't get myself to finish—stupid thought. No, I don't wanna know.

'You know I do,' she answers my incomplete question.

Her words take me by surprise, making my adrenaline rush at the speed of lighting as I pull her to my lips.

'I do too.'

Chapter 28

"Did He Not Tell You?"

Rashika

I wake up to an empty bed the following day. Recalling the events of last night makes my body ignite in ecstasy as I roll onto my side.

I remember falling asleep in Veer's arms while he ran his long fingers through my tangled hair. His smell still lingers on my pillow, but he isn't here. I jump from my bed and look around the room. The racket is lying near the window. So it wasn't a dream. He *was* here. I come back to bed and look through my bedside for a note or something. I lift the pillows and blanket. Nothing. He left without a word. If he wasn't comfortable staying the night, he could have just woken me and said so. I wouldn't have forced him to stay. Even a one-line chit would have sufficed! But no, he chose to secretively disappear while I was still asleep.

I thought that things between us were finally going well, that we finally understood each other better. Then why did he leave like that?

Did something happen? Did I say something wrong? Did last night not mean as much to him as it did to me?

He has a lot of explaining to do when I see him in college today. But last night was so intimate. Oh God, please don't make me act weird around him!

I grab a pair of fresh clothes from the cupboard and shower. Within fifteen minutes, I'm all dressed and ready to leave. We have an important test this morning, and I must meet Veer and clear my head before class. I can't be late. I arrange books in my bag, as I climb down the stairs. English. Check. Political Theory. Check. I've forgotten to add my map book. *Great.* In my frenzy, I skip the last stair and stumble. *Ughh.* I am SO distracted!

Grabbing a butter-toast from the dining table, I head out. Mom and Dad are sitting in the verandah. Mom is pouring tea while Dad is busy reading The Indian Herald. I notice a big empty space instead of the editorial column on the newspaper's first page.

It is an interesting feeling to greet them this particular morning, knowing that I had a boy hidden in my room only a few hours ago. I blush awkwardly as I turn around and head to the Ambassador.

On my way to college, my eyes fall on the narrow road leading to the dargah of Hazrat Nizamudin Auliya. I see devotees with beautiful white and green *chunnis* making their way towards the *dargah*. I pray to the *Mushkil Kusha* saint to protect Veer's father and to give his family strength. Just as I open my eyes, an idea strikes me. I manage to talk with Prem Uncle about my idea without the nagging (but necessary) presence of Pahalwan ji.

I don't think I've ever been more terrified or eager to reach college. But all my eagerness goes down the drain when I cross the bike parking and find Veer's usual spot empty. I see Imran, Abhimanyu and a few others standing there, smoking cigarettes. I check my wristwatch. 8:21 AM. The test starts in nine minutes.

Is he not coming or what?

I'm losing my patience.

Hesitantly, I decide to walk towards the boys. Maybe they know something I don't.

'Hi,' I say, as they pass questioning glares at me. 'Is Veer coming today?'

I ask as normally as possible, ignoring the possibility of me being the last person he spoke with yesterday.

Imran is utterly disinterested, as expected. Abhimanyu looks like he is contemplating whether he should answer me or not.

'When did you become such a stalker?' Imran opens his useless mouth. I ignore him.

'If you know something, tell me!' I turn to Abhimanyu, 'Please,' I add.

The guys pass grins amongst themselves. There goes my self-respect.

'Veer took the morning train to Lucknow. He's taking aunty to his grandparent's house,' Abhimanyu answers.

Lucknow! Did Gaytari Aunty make up her mind about uncle? Or is it because Veer wants her to stay safe and away from Delhi? I don't understand.

'Did he not tell you?' Abhimanyu asks, observing my confused expressions.

'Umm, yes, of course, he did...it...it slipped my mind,' I make a failed attempt at saving face.

'Sure he did,' Imran jokes as I thank Abhimanyu and head inside the building, feeling more embarrassed than I should.

Veer never tells me what he is up to! I know he's not obligated to. It's not like I'm his girlfriend or anything. But it'd be nice to not be in the dark, for once. All his friends knew. I was the only one who didn't.

I enter class. 8:28 AM. Students have already started sitting as per their roll numbers. Veer's seat is still empty.

Does Veer not have enough faith in me to tell me? He did tell me things yesterday, but why not this? My thoughts seem to be stuck.

I take my seat.

Maybe he forgot to. Maybe I'm overthinking it.

This boy really messes with my mind!

Professor Mehta enters and begins to dictate questions.

Rashika! Test. Focus!

Chapter 29

"Of Course, It Can't Be You"

Veer

My weary eyes stare out from the berth window, into the wilderness, as the Rajdhani express travels past the northern countryside.

On the outskirts of villages, wheat fields shine like gold in the moonlight, reminding me of Rashika. Images of her lying on the grass at the Teen Murti gardens...lying in my arms just four nights ago...consume my conscience as I doze off, dreaming of us, together in outfields of gold.

The train arrives in Delhi at 7:45 AM. For the first time in my life, returning to Delhi feels like returning to a hostile home with no family.

Mom is in Lucknow now, safe from the madness lying ahead. And who knows where Dad is! But no matter how much everyone back in Lucknow wanted me to transfer to Banaras University and stay with them, I know I must be here, in Delhi...to finish what I started, and also because...I...I can't go that long without seeing Rashika, who I fear wouldn't want to see me.

But how do I tell her that I had to do what I did! Not because sneaking out while it was still dark was the most practical thing to do, but because I am not strong enough.

I couldn't bear seeing the first faint wisps of the morning sun flickering across her cheek. I couldn't handle her delicate eyelids fluttering in the teasing sunlight, making her pull the blanket and drool over me as she rolled to her side.

I couldn't leave knowing whether she called out my name in her sleep.

As much as I hated keeping things from Rashika, I had to keep her out of my mess. The less she knew, the better. Rashika couldn't be a liability.

And so I waited till she fell asleep, watching her and taking in everything...her smell...her skin...her soft snores...everything that will get me through the rest of my nights.

I get off the coach to find Imran waiting for me at the platform, bearing good news. He guards my suitcase as I quickly freshen up in the station restrooms. We'll be driving straight to Hindu. Today is an important day at college. I need to be there to see how the events unfold and manipulate them if need be.

I'm standing by the blackboard, borrowing notes

from the girl who sits behind me when Rashika enters the English classroom. The immediate relief on her face upon seeing me in class makes me choke mid-sentence.

But the relief is short-lived. An unnecessary emotion takes over as she watches me talk with another girl. She does know she is the only one, right?

'Jealous?' I tease, walking to her. *God, why did I say that!*

'You wish,' she sneers, taking her seat.

Damn right, I wish.

Do you know what else I wish? To pull you behind the open door of this classroom, pin you against the wall and kiss you till you gasp for air.

That's what I wish.

I walk up to my seat and bury my head into the literature book as Professor Sharma begins her lecture.

Some time into the lecture, a student enters the class and whispers something to the Professor.

'Students who are a part of The Hindu Daily need to report to the principal's office right now,' Professor announces.

Oh.

The whole way down from our class to the admin block, Rashika walks ahead of me, ignoring my presence altogether. Not a single word is exchanged.

Most of the newspaper staff is already inside when we walk into the Principal's office. Every second person's eyes are fixed on the copy of The Daily in their hands. Others are cluelessly staring at each other. Siddharth looks like someone just told him he's an adopted child.

I ask one of the reporters standing near the pile of newspapers to pass a copy to me and read the headline on the front page.

COMPULSORY STERILIZATION DRIVE TO BEGIN BY END OF THE YEAR

Centre to forcefully drag rural poor to surgery irrespective of age and marital status

By Anonymous.

Oh.

No doubt everybody is freaking out.

'I have received a call from the press office. They're shutting down the paper,' Principal Bhatia informs once he is done reading the article. 'There are not many newspapers circulating in Delhi right now; your exposé has blown up!' He shakes his head in disappointment. 'The government is not happy. They want the name of the student responsible...they will not rest until I give them a name.'

'But sir-' Siddharth defends, but the Principal is not in the mood to listen.

'Siddharth, I thought you were a responsible student! How could you let this blunder happen under your watch!' The Principal's temperature rises as our faces drop below sea level, 'Did I not warn you, specifically—DO

NOT PUBLISH ANYTHING even *remotely* against the government!! Now the entire city has read this!' he slams his copy on the desk. 'You stupid children, do you even know how serious this is! It's no joke! The student who did this could go to jail for sedition!'

'I-I personally vet every article...two times, sir! Once, before sending it to the censors and then after making the changes they ask for! I did that yesterday afternoon too...like always...the article wasn't there in the folder then...I don't kn-' Sid is on the verge of cracking. 'I do not know...how it ended up going to the printers!'

One by one, the Principal interrogates each of us, asking if we knew who was behind the article. As if the person who knew or wrote it would admit the truth!

'Of course, it can't be you,' he says when he reaches Rashika.

Obviously.

'Sir, I was in Lucknow. I haven't attended college for the past four days,' I answer when he asks me, 'My leave application is with the Registrar. You can confirm with him if you like.'

Chapter 30

"Because I'm An Idiot"

Rashika

State-sponsored population control...targeting underprivileged...poor rural men to be forced onto the operating table—whether or not they want the vasectomy, whether or not they have children.

I quickly read through the article as Principal sir lashes out at Siddharth and the department heads.

Wait a second...this style...this format...seems familiar...my suspicion rises with each line.

Sanjay Gandhi's gruesome political campaign... government workers to get monthly sterilisation quotas... sterilisation certificate necessary for government job...free medical treatment...

Oh my God. He wrote this. *Veer* wrote this! This is his writing style! The word choice. The satirical tone. The judgmentalism! I have read every article Veer has written so far...the super long sentences, too many commas! It's definitely him!

Siddharth edits ten articles a day; he can miss it...but I...I know for sure. Veer Pratap Singh is 'Anonymous'.

But he was in Lucknow…then how did he…?

I keep my eyes buried in the paper for the entirety of Principal sir's rebuke, too scared that if my eyes meet Veer's, then my pale face might give it away for everyone to know.

I hasten to catch up to Veer as he climbs the stairs back to our Political Theory class.

'You might have fooled everyone in there...' I confront, appearing in his way, '...but you cannot fool me!'

'I don't know what you're talking about,' he denies, moving aside.

'And I don't know how you got that information or managed to get it published, but I know it's you who did it!' I assert in his ear, stopping him by his wrist.

'Stay away from me,' he grunts, freeing his wrist from my hold and continuing up the stairs.

'NO.' I protest, obstructing him. He grabs my arm. 'What the hell, Veer!'

Students in the corridor are staring at us as he pulls me through the corridor.

'People are watching! What's wrong with you?'

'Get in,' he orders, pushing open the storeroom door at the end of the corridor.

'What-'

He bolts the door shut, switching on the lights.

'What's your problem, huh?' he advances toward me.

'*My* problem?! *You* wrote that article! Did you not?!'

'Yes, I did!' he bellows, 'So what?'

'Did you not hear the Principal?' I yell back, 'The government is looking for the reporter, Veer! Have you even considered what'll happen if they know you did this?!'

'I don't care!'

'You have to, Veer! This is dangerous. Think about Aunty! How will she feel if you are arres-' I'm unable to complete my sentence. It's too hard to even think about. 'No...you have to be careful. You must stay off the radar. Do absolutely nothing…' I pace back and forth '...how did you get it through the censors!?'

'Imran. I gave him the article before leaving for Lucknow,' he answers, seeing the worry on my face. 'He arranged the key to the newsroom and added it to the file of approved articles after Sid vetted them and left.'

'You told him. Imran knew, all along!' I shake my head in disbelief, a pool of disappointment brimming in my eyes. 'But you didn't bother telling me…you didn't trust me...after all that we-'

'I didn't tell you because I knew you'd react this way... and talk me out of it!' he defends himself, 'I had to do this...I had to do this for my dad!'

'You think this is what your Dad wants?' I scoff, 'For you to join him in jail?!'

'They can't arrest me. They have no proof.'

'They DON'T need proof! Don't you understand? You're...you're Vikram Pratap Singh's son! Working at The Daily! That is all the proof they'll need!' I rationalise. 'I would've warned you if you'd told me that night. But no, you just chose to disappear on me!'

'That's what you're really angry about? Me disappearing? Isn't it?'

'I'm angry about everything, Veer! You make me mad... SO mad! I-I can't even look at you right now!' I chew the insides of my cheeks, avoiding bursting into sobs.

I hate the way he makes me feel.

'If that's the case, then why are you still standing in front of me? Why don't you go and tell them I did it... go and tell everything...to Siddharth…the Principal...the police' he challenges, drawing nearer. 'Why not let them take me...let me rot in jail! That way, you'd never have to see me again!'

'I can't!' I shout, but the voice coming out is small and cracking. 'You know I can't!'

'WHY?'

Because I'm in love with you damn it! I love you very very much!

'Because I'm an idiot!' I scream as he reaches his hands to my wet cheeks. His face is inches away from mine, and suddenly I'm aware that I'm breathing too hard. 'A complete idiot!' I cry, shoving his chest and pushing him back against the wooden almirah.

In a jiffy, Veer grabs my hands in his fists and pulls me to his lips.

Before I know it, his strong arms are wrapped around my waist, squeezing me against his chest as I begin to thread my fingers through his hair and tug harder. His hands move smoothly over my back and I find myself unable to stop. His tongue slides into my mouth like it is his gateway to freedom, and I feel my body melt into his.

Oh no…no...wait...we can't be doing this!

Rashika break the kiss! Please. NOW.

I force myself to pull back and break away from his touch, catching him completely off guard.

'Rashika…?' His startled voice is thick and raspy through his swollen lips. I step back, clasping my hands over my mouth.

'I told you!' I sniffle, my tears appearing 'told you...to stay away from me! I told you...but you didn't listen...you never listen to me!' I sob and storm out of the storeroom.

Veer comes after me, calling my name. I run into the girl's washroom. The janitor stops Veer from entering behind me. Locking myself in one of the stalls, I weep as I hear his footsteps disappear.

Chapter 31

"If Something Happens To You.."

Rashika

11:30 AM.

Professor Mehta assigns us a sixty-page reading of the Rule of Law and dismisses the class. I'm placing books in my bag when Veer barges in through the door. Dodging the students heading out of the classroom, he is towering at my desk before God grants my wish to become invisible.

'You need to go home. Right now!' He instructs, blocking my way as I desperately try to move past him. 'I've got information...the article...the situation has escalated...the opposition is going to stage a protest on campus at 12. You must not be here!'

'You have no right to tell me what to do!' I fake a brave front, my insides quivering with the news.

'Rashika, listen to me, this is not the time to argue... the police will arrive any moment now... and the situation will get out of hand. You MUST leave!' he stresses. 'I've asked your bodyguard. He's at the reception, calling your house. Prem Uncle should be here to pick you up soon.'

'But-'

'Rashika! No buts. Just listen to me this one time…' he begs, caressing his thumb over my cheek. 'I can't...if something happens to you...because of me...I-' he chokes.

'Fine! I'll leave,' I concur, removing his hand from my face. 'But you promise me...you'll leave too! You have to Veer...the police...you're an easy target.'

'I know,' he shakes his head, 'I'll leave…in time.' His resolute expression gives away that nothing I say will convince him otherwise.

'Take care of yourself.' I plead. Tears beginning to surface in my eyes at the possibility of Veer being...no. No! He'll be alright.

'I will.' He gives me a smile that doesn't meet his eyes and backs off.

I force myself to walk out into the corridor but can't help peeking back inside the classroom window.

Veer is still there, leaning over my desk. His fidgety hands run amok through his hair as he tries to gather himself together.

I make a life-altering decision right there and then.

12:30 PM.

As Prem Uncle and Pahalwan ji escort me from the Principal's office to the back gate of Hindu, I see nothing but chaos. Police vans and constables. Students in handcuffs. Remains of burning effigies. Dawdling smoke of tear gas. Broken glass bottles, batons, and stones. Barricades and barbed wires.

And I know I did the right thing.

Chapter 32

"It's My Turn Now"

Veer

The morning after the protest, Hindu College feels awfully quiet. Classes are half-empty and Professors are on leave. Canteen is bereft of chatter.

Even as I run laps around the cricket ground, I find no students sitting in the sun, bunking classes. No couples beneath the stands. No athletes practicing, teammates cheering, coaches screaming. Only silence—the kind that comes before a deadly storm. But it is too late for me to steer my ship back to shore. My ship has sailed and is bound to sink.

My grandfather, freedom fighter Prithvi Pratap Singh, went to jail. My father, opposition leader Vikram Pratap Singh, *is* in jail. I, irrational teenager Veer Pratap Singh, am next in line.

I may have been among the lucky protestors who escaped the police, but it is only a matter of time before they come for me, and when they do, I will go with my head held high. I am not a coward who'd hide underground and let them hound the people I love.

Mom and Dad will be hurt when they know, but at least they'd be proud, which isn't something I can say for Rashika. She may not see why I did what I did right now, but she will one day. And I wish that day she is willing to forgive me.

'Veer...wait!' Naina calls at me. 'Why are you running in the sun? You'll faint!'

I have lost count of the number of laps I've run. My T-shirt is soaking in sweat, and my face is red due to the heat. My legs tremble, and my stomach aches, but the pain I'm inflicting on my body isn't helping numb the pain in my heart. It hurts me to hurt her. And it hurts bad.

'No reason,' I breathe, stopping as Naina reaches me.

'Here...' She gives me her water bottle as I wipe off the sweat from my forehead.

'Thanks!' I take a sip and realise just how dry my throat is. 'If you're looking for Imran, he's not here.'

'I was looking for you, actually.'

'Why? Has Rashika come?' Tadpoles dance in puddles of hope in my imagination.

'No. Of course not!'

The puddles dry up, and the toads die.

'Has she talked to you? Will she come tomorrow?' I

ask, knowing the answer.

There's no chance Chaudhary would let her come to this minefield of a campus, and I agree with him for a change. But still, I'd hoped to see her when I walked into class, to bump into her as I climbed down the stairs, and whirled past corridors. I had hoped she'd find me in the nets and pick a fight with me.

But she was nowhere. Hope is such a bitch.

'Tomorrow?' Naina sounds confused, 'It's only the first day today. Her suspension's for another thirteen days!'

'Suspension?'

'Yeah! Rashika's suspension...she got suspended for two weeks, right? For the article she wrote...I still can't believe she went against her father and his government like this! That's so unlike her!'

'Suspension...article...what the hell are you saying?' I coax, my voice quaking as I put the pieces together.

'Oh I-I thought you knew.'

'Knew what?!'

Rashika can't. No, she didn't! Did she?

'She-umm-'

'Tell me, damn it!' I spiral '...no...sorry...I'm sorry... just tell me...please...Naina, I have to know!'

'Rashika is the one who wrote the sterilisation exposé Veer!' she gives in, 'Principal Bhatia suspended her immediately when he found out! Her Dad is handling it...but please don't tell anyone!'

'She-she...what?!' I bury my head in my hands, a

vacuum of guilt and despair sucking the air around me.

Why did she have to do this? Why?

I want to scream into the emptiness; scream at myself, scream at her!

It's all my fault. I clench my hair, cursing the moment I decided to meet with that party worker at Rajan tea stall! I should never have taken that file. I should have never written that article...shit.

'Veer...are you alright?' Naina asks. I nod, lying. 'Look, I don't know what is going on with you two...but you mean something to Rashika. You're pretty much all she talks about! Veer said this. Veer did that. It's always about you! So whatever it is, you need to sort it out!'

From her reaction, I doubt if Rashika has told her the whole story...the *real* story. If she had, Naina would be punching me in the gut right now for the pain I've caused Rashika. Even I would punch me.

'She asked me to give you this...' She takes out an envelope from her bag. 'Hope this helps,' Naina says with a sympathetic smile and leaves, giving me privacy.

I stagger to the stands, opening the envelope with trembling fingers.

What else is left to say now? No reasoning Rashika can offer will allow me to let her take the blame for me. These are my actions, and I will pay the price for them.

A chit.

You did what you had to. It's my turn now.
The investigation is closed. Do not try to sabotage it.

Yours,
Rashika.

A letter.

Dearest Veer,
I am writing to you from my cell in Tihar jail.

Despite my past actions, I understand that you and your mother are concerned about me. There is no need to worry. I am with the other political prisoners from the party, and we all are doing fine. We are here in preventive detention, with no means to challenge our arrests. Therefore, I need you to make peace with the fact that there is no way out for me until the Emergency continues.
This might be the last time you're hearing from me for a while. We are not allowed any contact or visitors.

Rashika beti may be kind enough to extend this favour in the future too, and I cannot thank her enough, but I cannot risk your safety by asking you to write to me.

I do not know how to say this, or if any words will ever make up for the mistakes I have made, but I am sorry. I am so sorry for wronging you and your mother and not being the man you both deserve. I deeply regret my behaviour and am utterly disappointed in myself. I know I am not worthy of your forgiveness but I promise you, not as a politician but as your father, that I am ready to do whatever it takes to win you both back.

Prison is no less than a rehabilitation camp, and my time here is the punishment I deserve for my ill karma. Being locked alone has given me the time to introspect and make amends. Today is my sixteenth day being sober. It is difficult, but the hope of being reunited with my family keeps me going. I will plead for your acceptance only after I have overcome my addiction and learned to control my anger. I also do not know if your mother will ever give our family and me a second chance, but I will respect her decision. Veer, promise me that you will be by your mother's side. You must take care of your mother, and you cannot do that if you continue putting yourself under the government's radar. I was slipped a copy of the article you wrote in The Hindu Daily. An excellent piece of journalism indeed. I was impressed by your understanding of the complexities of politics. You are the one who will keep our family legacy alive, not me. But you must not be impulsive. I do understand why you felt the need to retaliate publicly and expose their misdeeds. I am happy that you, my son, have the courage to stand up against oppression. I was right in naming you Veer. You have grown up to be a brave and brilliant man!

But I need your word that you will try your best to avoid being caught and never pull off something like this again, especially when I am not there to protect you.

You have the spark of a great leader. We will use it wisely in elections, not to encourage protests which end in young students like you landing in jail. Being locked up behind bars, you can change nothing, not this time. But being outside, you can make a difference. You can be my eyes and ears to the world outside. Plan ahead with the members left of the opposition. They will contact you themselves when the time comes. Meanwhile, lay low and contribute discreetly. In politics, people will use you as a pawn and then throw you away. You must play smart and not let yourself be used. You have to stay safe. Stay strong.

Believe in democracy. Believe in fighting fairly.

The Emergency cannot go on forever and is bound to end one day, and when it does, the public will rule once again, and you, my son will have played a greater role in its realisation than any of us stuck inside.

I am so proud of you son!

Love,

Dad

Chapter 33

"For Him, Anything"

Rashika

'I am highly disappointed in you Rashika. I took you for an intelligent girl. But you let yourself be manipulated so easily!' Dad lectures me in his study.

'Have you learnt nothing from being my daughter? You should be the one to manipulate others! Not the other way round! You do not lie to your father and join a cult newspaper behind his back! You do not go around writing seditious articles! You do not fall for political propaganda and turn against your father's government!'

Dad is right. I did get manipulated. But not by some political propaganda. I got manipulated by the cosmic propaganda called love. Cosmic propaganda made me fall for Veer Pratap Singh and pushed me to take the fall for him.

'I am sorry, Dad. I should have been careful.'

'I have settled the matter with the Principal and the censors. It will stay hidden. No record,' he informs, considering my apology. 'You should be happy that I am your father! Otherwise, you would be in Tihar right now!'

Power does bring privileges. Just like I had calculated, Principal sir had called Dad, not the police. When you are the daughter of the Finance Minister, people are more willing to give you the benefit of the doubt. You have closed-door conversations and settlements to save you from being thrown into prison.

I could get away with being caught.

But the law is not the same for everyone. If caught, Veer would be arrested. He wouldn't get a lawyer or be bailed out of prison. He would face sedition charges which would reduce his whole identity to this one horrible experience.

I will not let that happen. I will not let him ruin his life.

He will stay safe and free. Naina will give him the letter Prem Uncle arranged. He will listen to his father, if not me, and he will be okay.

'Thank you!' I mumble.

'I told them you were brainwashed, and it clouded your judgement,' Dad states, 'I never expected this from you Rashika! You made me look like a fool in front of my colleagues! Where did you even get that information? Who have you been talking to?'

'It was my choice, Dad. No one forced me into anything...*I* want to be a journalist...cover challenging stories, report the truth,' I confess, 'I disagree with what your government is doing, and there is nothing wrong in speaking against it. We live in a democracy, do we not?'

I never thought I'd be able to confront Dad, but the fear of him grilling me for answers about the article gives me sudden courage. He must believe I did this. He can never know the truth.

'These are strange times Rashika. You are not thinking straight. You're confused. You do not know what you are saying!'

'I do! I was just too afraid of you to say it out loud!'

'This college has derailed you! You lie, cheat, plan and plot! You argue!' Dad's brows wrinkle in an angry frown. 'This is not my daughter. My daughter is responsible and obedient! My daughter respects me!'

'I respect you, Dad. I do. But your good girl is tired of being good! I am-'

'This would never have happened if I'd sent you to England,' he shakes his head. 'I wanted to hear your side of the story, give you a chance to explain. But I'd made up my mind the moment your Principal told me. You will no longer study at Hindu. I have made some calls for you at Cambridge. You will complete your degree there. In peace. Away from all this nonsense.'

Seven thousand, five hundred and fifty-four kilometers—the distance between Delhi and London. The minimum distance needed to ensure Veer doesn't come knocking at my window, and I don't run away with him when he does.

I lie flat on my back. The white ceiling is a screen projecting films from my mind's eye.

Veer and Rashika. Nine years old. Returning from school. Listening to *Geetmala*. Playing cricket. Laughing. Running. Eavesdropping.

Veer and Rashika. Nineteen years old. Debating in classrooms. Passing chits. Stealing glances. Typing articles. Riding a bike. Bunking college.

Hiding. Fighting. Crying.

Kissing.

My longing gaze shifts to the window, staring into an abyss of nothingness.

The one thing I can't have is the thing I want the most.

We do not choose who we fall in love with. But we do choose how we act about it.

If letting him go is the sacrifice I have to make to save him, then that is how I choose to love him.

For him, anything.

Chapter 34

"We'll Get In Trouble Together"

Prem

'Namaste Sahib,' I salute as Sahib comes out to the driveway. Rashika treads behind him; her head fixed on the concrete.

I'm driving them to Hindu College. They will collect her documents, sign some papers, and she will be ready to leave.

I will never be driving her to college again.

I remember the first time Memsahib sent me to pick Rashika and Veer from their school.

It was a foggy day in December. The sky was overcast with clouds, and chilly winds were blowing. I'd switched on the Ambassador's heater on my way to Barakhamba to make sure *baccha log* didn't feel cold when they got in the car. The roads were hazy with mist. Traffic was slow and I was running late.

When I'd finally reached school, Rashika and Veer weren't at the gate. I'd gotten down and hastily scanned the area for two kids of the same height with identical backpacks, and there they were at the general store down the road.

'Ice Cream! In this weather!' I exclaimed, pacing to them. Their orange bars freeze to their mouths as they see me. Perhaps they were expecting their usual driver Shyam, not me, the new recruit. I'd only been recently transferred to Chaudhary Sahib, and from what I knew, these two little devils spent every waking hour either making a nuisance or getting scolded for it.

'Uncle, please don't tell our parents,' Rashika made a doll face.

I was attached to Aksai Chin during the Indo-China war of 1962. My experience watching for enemies at the border is A1. But my experience watching kids is zero. I wasn't sure what to do in such a situation.

'You might fall ill *beta ji*!' I shook my head, taking them to the car. 'I need to tell Sahib.'

'Prem Uncle, please don't tell them!' Tiny Veer appeared in front of my towering silhouette, 'If you want you can tell my mom, I'll get scolded...but please don't tell Gaytri Aunty or Amar Uncle anything...he's very strict!'

Standing up for your partner in crime—that's a trait even us policemen admire.

'Veer, no...' Rashika interrupted. 'We ate ice cream together. We'll get in trouble together.'

These two were thick as thieves. Who was I to rat them out?

That day we made a pact. A pact that stands to date—

What happens on Prem Uncle's watch, stays with Prem Uncle.

⁂

Laila-Majnu, Mirza-Sahiban, Shirin-Farhad. The greatest loves of all time are all over now.

Who knew that the two naughty little kids bouncing and giggling in the back of the Ambassador would face the fate of the tragic folklores of our time.

Rashika-Veer. Two names that once echoed as one at Akbar road.

Veer-Rashika. Two playmates who were perfect for each other. One would pull a prank, and the other's puppy eyes would get them out of trouble. One would swing the bat and break a window, and the other's crying face would compel the neighbours to return their ball. One would get caught, and the other would step up to take the fall.

Rashika-Veer. The sky and the sun. The salt and the sea.

The Yin and the Yang, one complementing the other, completing the other.

The feud between their fathers can make them hide it all they want, but nothing escapes my soldier's eyes.

I've observed them around each other. I've seen Rashika tuck her hair or squeeze the strap of her sling bag as we reach the college gates every morning. I've seen

Veer straighten his shirt and adjust his hair in his bike's mirror when Rashika gets out of the car.

I had noticed her walk past him as if they'd never met, and Veer puffing his cigarette like oxygen in response. I've noticed Veer's bike parked at a different spot the same day Rashika was suddenly wearing jhumkas after college. But as always, their secrets are safe with their Prem Uncle.

When Veer had asked if Rashika's room was still the same one, I'd nodded. If it were someone else, he would have had a good taste of the police *lathi* instead. Veer is different. I saw the way he'd kissed her forehead after getting her out of the protest and handing her safely to me. It was love, not lust. So when she asked me to help find Pratap Sahib's jail cell and get a letter for Veer, I couldn't refuse. I owe them at least this.

The convoy stops outside the administration block. Sahib and Rashika both walk-in accompanied by security details. I and the others on duty wait outside by the car.

Within minutes, the news of Rashika coming to campus reaches Veer, and he comes frantically looking for her.

'Let him through,' I direct the security detail wrestling him as he tries to get past security.

'Where is she?' he asks desperately, running to me.

'Inside, with the Principal.'

'Why?'

Veer has been coming outside the house every night since Rashika's suspension. Without fail, he'd park his bike on the road opposite number 15 and sit there staring at the light coming from Rashika's room until it was turned off.

'Prem Uncle...why?' His trembling voice begs me to answer.

I tell him that Chaudhary Sahib has made up his mind. Rashika is leaving for England, and she is not coming back to Hindu.

The earthquake in Veer's voice turns into a violent tsunami of tears in his eyes. The security details watch confusedly as the star-crossed lover kicks the floor and screams silently into the sky.

They don't know who he is. They don't know the reason behind his misery. If they did, this poor boy wouldn't be standing here.

I put my hand on his shoulder. If it were up to me, I'd drive him and Rashika to the airport instead.

Moments later, Rashika appears with a file in her hand. Sahib is busy conversing with the Principal and staff who have come to see him off.

There is a visible effort in Rashika's steps as her eyes tie with Veer's, and she resists the invisible string that pulls her to him. But the more she tries to break away, the more the string seems to tighten around her throat, choking her words as her tears reappear.

They do not speak, but their eyes do. They meet and fall and meet again; linger, look and sigh. Distance and duty, strength and sacrifice, all seem to be forgotten for a short while. In their eyes there is helplessness. There is anger. There is defeat. And there is love.

'Tell her...I love her, will you?' he sobs as Rashika trudges towards the car. 'I will *always* love her.'

'She wouldn't have done what she did if she didn't already know that.' I pat his back before rushing to open the backseat door for Sahib and Rashika.

As I drive out the college gates, the rearview mirror reflects Rashika's bloodshot eyes, and in the wing mirror, I see everything she is leaving behind. I see Veer clenching his hair and slowly falling to his knees as I turn the car onto the road.

I have witnessed this scene before. One of them leaving, and one of them being left behind.

Love does not know its own depth until the hour of separation.

Out beyond the lands of right and wrong,
there is a field.
I'll meet you there.

—Rumi

Epilogue

Veer

10 January 2020, Fitzrovia, London.

'I've approved the itinerary for the High Commission's Republic Day programme, but I've also suggested a few additions,' I hand over the file to my secretary. 'Tell the Ministers to go through them, and give me a call if they have any questions, especially about the seminar on the Indian Constitution.'

Once he leaves, I close my study door and move to the living room for my daily afternoon ritual.

Drops of winter rain are racing down the living room window. I raise the temperature of the electric fireplace. The crackling of fire merges with the sound of brewing coffee as I pour myself another cup.

Wearing my distance glasses, I switch on the TV. My wrinkled fingers are accustomed to pressing channel 231 on the remote. BBC World News.

It's almost time. Rashika's program will go on air any minute. She's interviewing a panel on the ongoing student protests in India today.

'Grandpa, Grandpa!' the main door barges open. Samara and Fateh are back from school. 'We're home!' They drop their umbrellas and boots at the entrance and run to me. I keep my coffee mug on the side table, next to the flowers I bring my wife every day, and take them both in my arms.

The title sequence of Rashika's program begins to play. I increase the volume as the kids pounce on the sofa, sitting on my either side.

'Shhh...it's starting...look...' I never tire of saying, '...your grandmother.'

Glossary

1971 War - The Indo-Pakistan War of 1971 was a military confrontation between India and Pakistan that occurred during the Bangladesh War of Independence in erstwhile East Pakistan from 3 to 16 December 1971.

1971/Fifth General Elections - Held in March 1971 instead of 1972. Congress (R) led by Indira Gandhi secured an overwhelming majority winning 352 out of 518 seats in the Lok Sabha. Congress (O) under Morarji Desai secured only 16 seats. With this, the Congress party led by Indira Gandhi established its claim to being the 'real' Congress and restored to it the dominant position in Indian politics.

ABVP - Akhil Bharatiya Vidyarthi Parishad is a right-wing all India student organisation affiliated to the Hindu nationalist Rashtriya Swayamsevak Sangh.

Adam Smith - Scottish economist and philosopher who came up with the theory of capitalism, ie. an economic system based on private ownership of the means of production and their operation for profit.

Allahabad High Court - on 12 June 1975, found Indira Gandhi guilty on the charge of misuse of government machinery for her election campaign in 1971 parliamentary elections. The court declared her election null and void and unseated her from her seat in the Lok Sabha. Also known as **Syndicate**. Started to fade away after 1971 General Elections.

BBC - British Broadcast Corporation.

Binaca *Geetmala* - A weekly countdown show of top filmi songs from Hindi cinema.

Black hole - A region of space-time where gravity is so strong that nothing—no particles or even electromagnetic radiation such as light—can escape from it.

Citizenship Amendment Act (Bill) protests - Also known as CAA Protest or CAB Protest, occurred after the Citizenship Amendment Act (CAA) was enacted by the Government of India on 12 December 2019. The move sparked widespread national and overseas ongoing protests against the act.

Communist Party of India (Marxist–Leninist) - Formed by the radicals within the Communist Party of India (Marxist) that advocated armed revolution and denounced participation in the electoral process. They mobilised a revolutionary peasants movement in Naxalbari, which evolved into an armed uprising.

Congress (O) - The Indian National Congress (Organisation) was a right-wing political party in India formed when the Congress party split following the expulsion of Indira Gandhi. Comprised of senior old leaders like K. Kamaraj, Morarji Desai and S. Nijalingappa.

Congress (R) - Indian National Congress (Requisitionists) was created in 1969; it was created and led by Indira Gandhi. After the landslide victory in 1971 General elections it came to be generally known as the 'New Congress'.

CPI - Communist Party of India, a leading left-wing national political party CPI (ML) saw Naxalbari as the spark that would start a new Indian revolution, and the movement came to be known as 'Naxalites' in several parts of India. The party got moral support from China, which actively encouraged the attempts of CPI (ML) to launch a revolution.

Dark Ages - A term for the Early Middle Ages or Middle Ages in the area of the Roman Empire in Europe, after its fall in the fifth century, characterising it as marked by economic, intellectual and cultural decline.

DMK - Dravida Munnetra Kazhagam, a political party based in south India.

Doon - The Doon School (informally Doon) is an all-boys highly selective boarding school in Dehradun, Uttarakhand.

DPS - Delhi Public School.

Garibi Hatao ('remove poverty') - The theme and slogan of Indira Gandhi's 1971 election campaign. The slogan and the proposed anti-poverty programs that came with it were designed to give Gandhi an independent national support, based on rural and urban poor.

Gulzarilal Nanda - A senior leader of Congress who was the Prime Minister of India for two short periods following the deaths of Jawaharlal Nehru in 1964 and Lal Bahadur Shastri in 1966. Both his terms ended after the ruling Congress's parliamentary leadership elections chose a new Prime Minister.

Gymkhana club - An exclusive membership club in New Delhi.

Habeas Corpus - A writ requiring a person under arrest to be brought before a judge or into court, especially to secure the person's release unless lawful grounds are shown for their detention. In India, Habeas Corpus is part of the Fundamental Right to constitutional remedies that were suspended during the Emergency.

Harappa - An archaeological site in Punjab, Pakistan. One of the largest settlements of the Indus Valley Civilization.

Hazrat Nizamudin Auliya - An Indian Sunni Muslim scholar, Sufi saint of the Chishti Order, and one of the most famous Sufis from the Indian Subcontinent.

High Commission - In the Commonwealth of Nations, a High Commissioner is the senior diplomat in charge of the diplomatic mission of one Commonwealth government to another. Instead of an embassy, the diplomatic mission is generally called a High Commissioner.

Indian National Congress - Major political party in India since 1885.

Indira Gandhi (1917 – 1984) - An Indian politician and a central figure of the Indian National Congress. She was the 3rd Prime Minister of India and was also the first and, to date, only female Prime Minister of India. Also refered to as Madam within the Congress. The daughter of Jawaharlal Nehru, the 1st Prime Minister of India. Indira Gandhi challenged the High Court's decision in the Supreme Court. Justice VR Krishna Iyer, on 24 June 1975, upheld the High Court judgement and ordered all privileges Gandhi received as an MP be stopped, and that she be debarred from voting. However, she was allowed to continue as Prime Minister pending the resolution of her appeal.

Jamaat-e-Islami - One of the original and most influential Islamist organisations, and the first of its kind to develop 'an ideology based on the modern revolutionary concept of Islam'.

Jawaharlal Nehru University - A public central university located in New Delhi, India.

Jayaprakash Narayan - Popularly referred to as JP or *Lok Nayak* ('People's leader'), was an Indian independence activist and political leader known for leading the mid-1970s opposition against Prime Minister Indira Gandhi, for whose overthrow he had called for a 'total revolution'.

Karl Marx - German economist and political theorist, came up with the theory of Communism, namely a socioeconomic order structured upon the ideas of common ownership of the means of production and the absence of social classes.

Lal Bahadur Shastri - Senior Congress leader, second Prime Minister of India, took over after Nehru.

Lutyens' Delhi - An area in New Delhi, India, named after the British architect Sir Edwin Lutyens (1869–1944), who was responsible for much of the architectural design and building during the period of the British Raj, when India was part of the British Empire in the 1920s, 1930s and 1940s.

Marx v/s Smith, or Communism vs Capitalism - Major ideological conflict of the modern world over the best and the most appropriate way of organising political, economic, and social life all over the world.

Mir Taqui Mir - An Urdu poet of 18th century Mughal India.

Morarji Desai - Senior Congress leader. Following the passing of Prime Minister Lal Bahadur Shastri, Desai was a strong contender for the position of Prime Minister, only to be defeated by Indira Gandhi. He was appointed as Deputy Prime Minister and Minister of Finance in Indira Gandhi's cabinet until 1969, when he resigned due to ideological difference with the PM.

MP - Member of Indian Parliament.

Nataraja idol - A statue depicting the Hindu god Shiv as the divine cosmic dancer. Built by Chola rulers.

Navnirman Andolan - (Re-invention or Reconstruction movement) A socio-political movement in 1974 in Gujarat by students and middle-class people against economic crisis and corruption in public life. It is the only successful agitation in the history of post-independence India that resulted in dissolution of an elected government of the state.

Naxalite - An extreme Maoist (far-left radical communist) group in India that originated in 1967 in West Bengal and which employs tactics of agrarian terrorism and direct action.

Parliamentary leadership elections - Secret Ballot Election within the Congress party to chose the leader who'd replace Shastri as Prime Minister.

Planning Commission - An institution in the Government of India, made after Independence which formulated India's Five-Year Plans (centralised and integrated national economic programs).

Plato - A political philosopher in Ancient Greece. Author of The Republic.

Prasar Bharati - India's largest public broadcasting agency, comprising the Doordarshan Television Network and All India Radio, which were earlier media units of the Ministry of Information and Broadcasting.

Prashasti - An Indian genre of inscriptions composed by poets in praise of their rulers.

Praveen Babi - Famous Bollywood actress in 1960-70s.

President rule in Gujarat and Bihar - Reference to student protests in the states under JP which resulted in the fall of state governments and imposition of President's rule (the suspension of state government and imposition of direct Union government rule in a state. Under Article 356 of the Constitution of India, in the event that a state government is unable to function according to Constitutional provisions).

Privy purse - In India, a privy purse was a payment made to the ruling families (Nawabs, Maharajas etc) of erstwhile princely states as part of their agreements to first integrate with India in 1947 after the independence of India, and later in 1949 to merge their states, thereby ending their ruling rights. The privy purses continued to be paid to the royal families until the 26th Amendment in 1971 by Indira Gandhi government, by which all their privileges and allowances from the central government ceased to exist, which was implemented after a two-year legal battle.

RK Laxman - An Indian cartoonist and political humorist, best known for his creation The Common Man and for his daily cartoon strip, 'You Said It' in The Times of India, which started in 1951.

Ram Manohar Lohia - An activist in the Indian independence movement and a major opposition leader against Congress rule.

Rashtriya Swayamsevak Sangh (RSS) - An Indian right-wing Hindu nationalist paramilitary volunteer organisation. The initial impetus was to provide character training through Hindu discipline and to unite the Hindu community to form a Hindu Rashtra (Hindu nation).

Right to Property controversy - In 1973, the Supreme Court gave a decision that has become very important in regulating the relations between the Parliament and the Judiciary since then. This case is famous as the Kesavananda Bharati case. In this case, the Court ruled that there is a basic structure of the Constitution and nobody—not even the Parliament (through amendment)—can violate the basic structure. The Court however later decided that the right to property (the disputed issue) was not part of the basic structure and therefore could be suitably abridged. Therefore, allowing Mrs Gandhi's government to implement its land reform program.

Rumi - A 13th-century Persian Sufi Poet.

S Nijalingappa - Senior leader of Congress, who was the Congress party President from 1968-69.

Sanjay Gandhi - Indian politician and the son of Indira Gandhi. In September 1976, Sanjay Gandhi initiated a widespread compulsory sterilisation programme to limit population growth. The exact extent of Sanjay Gandhi's role in the implementation of the programme is disputed, with some writers holding Gandhi directly responsible for his authoritarianism, and other writers blaming the officials who implemented the programme rather than Gandhi himself.

Sarita - Popular women's lifestyle magazine in hindi.

Socialist - Someone who believes in Socialism - political, social and economic philosophy of social/

government ownership of the means of production, and democratic control, such as workers' self-management of enterprises, subsidies etc.

Ten-point program - A radical socio-economic programme proposed by Indira Gandhi and adopted by the Congress Working Committee in May 1967. It focused on left-leaning, socialist measures. The meeting was held in Tashkent in the Uzbek Soviet Socialist Republic, Soviet Union (now Uzbekistan) from 4 to 10 January 1966 to try to create a more permanent settlement. The next day, Jayaprakash Narayan and Morarji Desai called for daily anti-government protests and organised a large rally in Delhi, where he said that a police officer must reject the orders of the government.

The Renaissance - A term used to describe a period of cultural rebirth in European history marking the transition from the Middle Ages to modernity and covering the 15th and 16th centuries. A distinguishing feature of Renaissance Art was its development of highly realistic linear perspective.

The Tashkent Declaration - A peace agreement between India and Pakistan signed on 10 January 1966 that resolved the Indo-Pakista War of 1965.

Total Revolution - A political movement initiated by students in the Indian state of Bihar in 1974 and led by the veteran Gandhian socialist Jayaprakash Narayan, popularly known as JP, against misrule and corruption in the state government. It later turned against Prime Minister Indira Gandhi's government in the central government. It was also called Sampoorna Kranti Movement and JP Movement.

USSR - The Soviet Union, officially the Union of Soviet Socialist Republics (USSR), was a socialist state that spanned Europe and Asia during its existence from 1922 to 1991.

VV Giri and 1969 Presidential Election - Fourth president of India from August 1969 to August 1974. He was the only President to be elected as an independent candidate. The election of a new President became a contest between the Prime Minister Indira Gandhi and the old guard of the Congress Party known as the Syndicate. The Congress Party decided to support Neelam Sanjiva Reddy as the presidential candidate, disregarding the Prime Minister's opposition. Giri, who was Vice President, resigned and decided to contest as an independent candidate. Prime Minister Gandhi then decided to support him, endorsing a 'vote of conscience' that allowed Congress legislators to vote for Giri who is regarded as the President who completely subordinated himself to the Prime Minister and has been described as a 'Prime Minister's President.'

Vijya Laxmi Pandit - Indian politician diplomat. First female governor, Nehru's sister.

Welham Girls' School - A private boarding school for girls located in Dehradun, Uttarakhand.

Acknowledgements

With all my love, I dedicate my second novel to my grandparents: my Dada, Shri TR Kalra, who laid the foundations of everything I aspire to be; my Dadi, Smt Veena Kalra, for introducing me to the world of imagination and storytelling; my Nanu, Shri BR Gupta, for being my first-hand guide and helping me capture the essence of India during the 1970s; and my Nani, Smt Sushma Gupta, for her endless positivity, energy and encouragement.

I cannot fully express my gratitude to my parents for being there for me every step of the way. My father, Shri Ranjeet Kalra, for always supporting me and my dreams. Thank you for making me believe that anything is possible.

My mother, Smt Deepti Kalra, for keeping me accountable and driven. Thank you for pushing me to be patient and persistent.

brother, Ruhaan Raj Kalra, for being my one. Thank you for being my biggest fan and ghest critic. You are my favourite human being on he planet.

A word of appreciation for my incredible friends, Ananya Sharma, Gardenia Kaushal and Mehar Singh for bearing with me and my initial drafts.

I am also extremely thankful to my alma maters, Presentation Convent School and Ashoka University, for nurturing my ability to express myself creatively.

My heartfelt gratitude to the team at Vitasta Publication: my publisher, Smt Renu Kaul Verma, my editor Shri Nitin Sathe and my copyeditor Miss Ridhima Gandhi. Thank you for giving young authors a platform to present their work.

Lastly, I am thankful to you, dear reader, for picking up this book and giving it life.